Acting Edition

I0589031

Lewiston / Clarkston

by Samuel D. Hunter

FOR PRODUCTION INQUIRIES

UNITED STATES AND CANADA
info@concordtheatricals.com
1-866-979-0447

UNITED KINGDOM AND EUROPE
licensing@concordtheatricals.co.uk
020-7054-7298

Each title is subject to availability from Concord Theatricals Corp., depending upon country of performance. Please be aware that *LEWISTON / CLARKSTON* may not be licensed by Concord Theatricals Corp. in your territory. Professional and amateur producers should contact the nearest Concord Theatricals Corp. office or licensing partner to verify availability.

This work is published by Samuel French, an imprint of Concord Theatricals Corp.

Part One, *LEWISTON*, premiered in New Haven, Connecticut at the Long Wharf Theatre (Gordon Edelstein, Artistic Director) on April 6, 2016. The production was directed by Eric Ting, with set design by Wilson Chin, costume design by Paloma Young, lighting design by Matthew Richards, and sound design by Brandon Wolcott. The stage manager was Charles M. Turner III. The cast was as follows:

MARNIE . . . . .Arielle Goldman
ALICE . . . . Randy Danson
CONNOR . . . . .Martin Moran
FEMALE VOICE . . . . Lucy Owen

Part Two, *CLARKSTON*, premiered in Dallas, Texas at the Dallas Theater Center (Kevin Moriarty, Artistic Director) on December 3, 2016. The production was directed by Davis McCallum, with set design by Andrew Boyce, costume design by Jessica Pabst, lighting design by Eric Southern, and sound design by Stowe Nelson. The stage manager was Kirstin Jones. The cast was as follows:

JAKE . . . . Taylor Trensch
CHRIS . . . . .Sam Lilja
TRISHA . . . . Heidi Armbruster

LEWISTON / CLARKSTON premiered in New York City at the Rattlestick Playwrights Theater (Daniella Topol, Artistic Director) on October 10, 2018. The production was directed by Davis McCallum, with set design by Dane Laffrey, costume design by Jessica Wegener Shay, lighting design by Stacey Derosier, sound design by Fitz Patton, and dramaturgy by John M. Baker. The stage managers were Katie Young and Joanne Pan. The cast was as follows:

LEWISTON

MARNIE . . . . Leah Karpel
ALICE . . . . Kristin Griffith
CONNOR . . . . .Arnie Burton
FEMALE VOICE . . . . Heidi Armbruster

CLARKSTON

JAKE . . . . .Noah Robbins
CHRIS . . . . Edmund Donovan
TRISHA . . . . Heidi Armbruster

AUTHOR'S NOTES

Dialogue written in *italics* is emphatic, deliberate; dialogue in ALL CAPS is impulsive, explosive.

A slash (/) indicates an overlap in dialogue. Whenever a slash appears, the following line of dialogue should begin.

Ellipses (...) indicate when a character is trailing off. Dashes (–) indicate where a character is being cut off, either by another character or themselves.

Dialogue in [brackets] is implied, not spoken.

PART ONE: LEWISTON

CHARACTERS

MARNIE – early to mid-twenties, female
ALICE – early to mid-seventies, female
CONNOR – fifties, male
FEMALE VOICE

SETTING

A fireworks stand off of a rural highway just outside of Lewiston, Idaho, near the Snake River. There are a few rows of shelves modestly stocked with small, unexciting fireworks: small fountains, smoke bombs, poppers, sparklers, etc., all labeled with handwritten price tags. Nothing too large, aerial, or explosive. The stand itself is open-air; every now and then we hear the sound of a car passing on the highway. A small cashbox, a few coolers, a couple lawn chairs.

TIME

Early July

.

Darkness

(As the lights go to black, we begin to hear distant nature sounds – wind rustling through trees, birds, etc.)

(It all sounds distant and tinny, like an old recording.)

(After a moment or two, we hear:)

FEMALE VOICE. Okay! Well, this is –... So here I am.

(Pause.)

Fort Union, North Dakota. Of course this isn't where it *actually* started, in Wood River, but that's –. This is more reasonable, starting from here. It'll take me – six weeks? Something like that?

(We hear the sound of a passing truck, a horn honking.)

If I sort of plug my ears and squint so I don't see the highway across the river or the suspension bridge, I can sort of – just barely – imagine what it was like back then.

(Pause.)

Maybe.

(The sound of another passing truck. Pause.)

It's weird, the –... In a landscape this big it's easy to see how small you really are.

(Short pause.)

I didn't expect that.

(Silence. We hear a few breaths, and then suddenly:)

Okay, well here I go!

(Pause.)

FEMALE VOICE. Here I go.

(With a click the recording finishes, and lights rise on:)

Scene One

*(**CONNOR** stands, holding some notecards and a pen. **ALICE** sits on a lawn chair.)*

(They are watching a small fountain firework on top of a piece of particle board. The firework has just finished; it's smoldering pathetically.)

(Finally:)

ALICE. Is it done?

*(Pause. **CONNOR** looks at it, keeping his distance.)*

CONNOR. Yyyyyyyes.

(Pause.)

Yeah it's done.

(Pause.)

It's cute.

ALICE. That was awful.

CONNOR. I think it's cute.

ALICE. That makes me want to move to Canada.

(She gets up, grabbing a bucket half-full of water. She goes to the fountain, putting it in the bucket, then sits back down.)

*(**CONNOR** looks at the blank notecards.)*

(Silence.)

CONNOR. I mean it's –. We could say "kid-friendly"?

ALICE. Everything we have is kid-friendly. You couldn't blow a finger off with anything here if you *tried.*

(Another silence. The sound of a passing car. **ALICE** *and* **CONNOR** *look up, watch as the car passes them and disappears.)*

CONNOR. I'm running out of things to say, do you –? How would you describe it?

*(**ALICE** moves to a cooler, opening it.)*

ALICE. Oh I don't know.

CONNOR. *(Writing.)* "An...audacious shower of light."

ALICE. You're not using that word right.

CONNOR. Well then *you* / give me something, I don't know.

ALICE. *(Looking in the cooler.)* You drank my last Michelob Light, / didn't you?

CONNOR. "An *unabashed* shower of light." / That's what I'm putting.

ALICE. Connor I was saving the last Michelob Light for the afternoon, did / you –

CONNOR. I'll buy you more, *stop*, / it's not like you paid for it, I'm the one who buys all the stupid beer –

ALICE. I'm not going to even bother carrying them all the way from the house if you're going / to steal them.

CONNOR. *(Going to a box.)* Okay, let's do another one, there are five or six / new fountains, I think.

ALICE. If you're gonna just light all the merchandise then we won't have anything left to sell.

CONNOR. We have to know what they do, you remember last year, no one bought anything because you couldn't tell them what any of them did.

ALICE. That's not why we didn't / sell anything.

CONNOR. We're only doing one of each, that's / not gonna break us –

ALICE. *We're not selling anything because no one wants these stupid little fireworks when they can just go to the damn reservation and buy whatever the hell they want, no one –...*

(Silence. She sits down.)

CONNOR. You okay?

ALICE. Yeah, I'm –...

> *(Pause.)*

He called again this morning.

CONNOR. Oh.

ALICE. Told me if I signed this week they'd give us one of the better condos. Near the pool.

> *(Pause.)*

CONNOR. I mean that's good, right? Pool?

> *(Pause.)*

We'll wait a couple more weeks, they'll up the offer.

ALICE. Mm-hm.

CONNOR. Just let me handle it. If they call again just come and get me, I'm better at this stuff than you are.

> *(Pause. He begins to root around in a box.* **ALICE** *looks out, spotting something.)*

ALICE. Look. That backhoe, there.

CONNOR. What?

ALICE. *The backhoe*, I said, that backhoe is on my property, they can't do that.

> *(***CONNOR*** *looks.)*

CONNOR. No, it's not.

ALICE. *Yes*, it is, the property line ends forty feet past the oak, / that doesn't –

CONNOR. Not past the oak, before the oak. Forty feet before the oak.

> *(Pause.* **ALICE** *looks.)*

ALICE. Are you *sure*?

CONNOR. Yes, Alice, I'm sure. That's not your tree anymore.

> *(Pause.)*

ALICE. Oh.

> *(She looks.* **CONNOR** *continues rooting through the box.)*

CONNOR. We got too much of everything, you know.

ALICE. Well if you have any ideas on how we're / gonna –

CONNOR. I don't have any ideas I'm just / saying –

ALICE. I could charge you rent, how about that? Living in my house for free, maybe I could make some money that way.

CONNOR. Oh for God's / sake.

ALICE. I'm just saying, I could probably pay the mortgage fine if I didn't have someone living in my house / rent-free.

CONNOR. When was the last time you went grocery shopping, can you tell me that?

ALICE. Okay you buy groceries, you buy the groceries.

CONNOR. *And* the cable.

ALICE. Oh and the cable, he's up on the cross now, he pays the cable.

> (**CONNOR** *goes to another box, starts rummaging around.*)

And you owe me for the cleaners, I got that black suit of yours cleaned.

CONNOR. What?

ALICE. I said I took your black suit to the cleaners yesterday which was nine bucks and / I –

CONNOR. I don't have a black suit.

ALICE. The one from the Men's Wearhouse, you know, with the –?

CONNOR. *(Still rummaging in the box.)* You mean that old charcoal grey suit? I haven't worn that in ten years, that thing / won't fit me anymore –

ALICE. Well what the hell else are you gonna wear?

CONNOR. I've got those black jeans and / I'll wear a dress shirt –

ALICE. *Jeans?* To a *funeral*?

CONNOR. *(Looking into the box.)* Oh no.

> (*Pause.* **ALICE** *looks at him.*)

ALICE. What?

CONNOR. Oh no. Oh, no.

ALICE. *What?*

>   *(**CONNOR** looks into the box.)*

CONNOR. It's a mouse. Mouse got / into it.

ALICE. *Goddam it.*

CONNOR. Chewed through five or six fountains.

ALICE. Which ones?

>   *(Pause. **CONNOR** looks.)*

CONNOR. Dragon Sunrise / Fountains.

ALICE. *Goddam it.*

>   *(**CONNOR** shakes the box.)*

It's still in there?

CONNOR. Yeah, it's –. It's dead. Thing's all bloated and gross, ate all that gunpowder, he's –. Oh, lord.

>   *(**MARNIE** enters, unseen by both **ALICE** and*
>   ***CONNOR**. She holds a duffel bag.)*

ALICE. What is wrong with these field mice?!

CONNOR. This construction on the development's making them go crazy, they don't know where to go, they just –. Oh he's not dead yet.

>   *(**ALICE** cringes.)*

ALICE. Just pull him out, put him out of his / misery.

CONNOR. I am *not* reaching in there, he's probably got plague.

>   *(Looking into the box.)*

Oh yep he's not dead yet, not dead at all. He's suffering though, gimme that [bucket of water] –

>   *(He looks up, sees **MARNIE**.)*

Oh, sorry –

>   *(**ALICE** sees **MARNIE**.)*

MARNIE. / I'm sorry –

ALICE. Oh –

CONNOR. That's fine, just didn't hear you pull up.

> (**ALICE** *goes to* **MARNIE**.)

ALICE. Don't mind us, we're just –. You looking for something in particular?

MARNIE. I –.

> (*Pause.*)

I'm just looking, I guess.

ALICE. Oh sure.

> (*She motions at* **CONNOR**, *who takes the box and exits.* **MARNIE** *begins looking around.* **ALICE** *hovers.*)

> (*She points to a variety box.*)

This is a nice value. Got everything you need there. Sparklers, little fountains, poppers. We throw in some jumping jacks with every purchase.

> (**MARNIE** *browses around a bit, looking at the fireworks. She picks one up.*)

That's a nice one.

MARNIE. What's, uh –. What's it do?

ALICE. Oh well let's see.

> (*She goes to the shelf, taking the label off.*)

(*Reading.*) "A brazen display" – dammit, Connor – "of red and green sparks with whistle at the end."

> (*Short pause.*)

Red and green with a whistle. It's good, it's a good one.

> (*Something on the shelf catches* **MARNIE**'s *eye; she looks at it.*)

Oh you like these?

> (**ALICE** *grabs it off the shelf.*)

The chickens, they're good. They squeal and shoot out sparks like they're laying eggs, kids love it.

(**MARNIE** *is looking at the firework, lost in thought.*)

You want one of the chickens?

(*Pause.* **MARNIE** *looks at her.*)

MARNIE. Sure, I guess.

ALICE. Okay then.

(*She takes one, takes it behind the cash register. She looks at* **MARNIE**, *who is lost in thought.*)

You okay, hon?

MARNIE. Yeah, I –.

(*Pause.*)

I used to come here when I was little.

ALICE. Oh yeah?

MARNIE. It's [different] –... I barely recognized it, I wasn't even sure this was the same place –

ALICE. Yeah, well it's changed quite a bit around here, if you were here that long ago. Whole town has really started to change.

(*Pointing.*)

All that construction is a new subdivision that they're trying to build, all this here.

MARNIE. Oh.

ALICE. I'm the only one left around here nowadays. Used to be me and the Davidsons, over there –

(*Pointing.*)

But they got offered some obscene amount of money, bought a house on the Oregon coast. You like sparklers at all?

MARNIE. What?

ALICE. We've got these Morning Glories, they're nice but they're not the best for little kids. You buying these for little kids?

MARNIE. No, I –

ALICE. Then you'd like the Morning Glories.

> *(She packs the sparklers in a bag with the chicken.)*

MARNIE. Are you going to sell your land too?

> *(Pause.)*

ALICE. Well, I –. I mean I've had to sell off most of it over the years, but I've still got my little patch here. Been in the family a long time.

> *(Pause.)*

I'm actually part of the Lewis family, you know like Lewis and Clark?

MARNIE. Oh.

ALICE. Yep. Meriwether Lewis was my great-great...great? ...grandpa's cousin. My great-great-grandpa started a cattle ranch here in the 1850s, stayed a cattle ranch for generations after that, up until thirteen, fourteen years ago.

MARNIE. What happened?

ALICE. Oh, you know. My husband passed, they opened that big slaughterhouse over in Orofino, and it –... Anyway.

> *(Pause.)*

The new subdivision here, they're actually naming it "Meriwether Terrace." I told them if Meriwether Lewis knew that his name was being attached to something like that, he probably would have stayed put on the East Coast, not even bothered coming out here and –

MARNIE. Are you going to sell them the rest of the land?

ALICE. Well, I –... I might have to, I –...

> *(Pause.)*

Doesn't matter anyway, it's just dirt when it comes down to it. You know the variety pack is really the best value.

> *(Pause.)*

MARNIE. I think I'm okay.

ALICE. Okay, well. Four nineteen, then. Make it an even four.

> (**MARNIE** *pulls out a wallet, takes out some cash*. **ALICE** *counts her change.*)
>
> (**MARNIE** *glances around nervously*. **ALICE** *looks at her.*)

Honey, did you –? Where's your car?

MARNIE. Oh, I –. I walked.

> (*Pause.*)

ALICE. You walked here *from town*?

> (**CONNOR** *re-enters with the box, which is now empty.*)

That's six miles! Listen, you don't want to walk all the way back to town, let Connor here give you a ride.

MARNIE. I'm fine –

ALICE. That's too long for someone to walk on the highway, / just let us –

CONNOR. You *walked* / here?

MARNIE. *I'm really fine.*

> (*She starts to walk away with her bag. Finally, she turns back to* **ALICE**.)

ALICE. Honey?

> (*Silence.*)
>
> (*She looks at* **MARNIE**, *recognizing her for the first time.*)

Oh –...

> (**CONNOR** *goes to* **MARNIE**.)

CONNOR. Miss, you okay?

MARNIE. I'm fine –

CONNOR. If you need a / phone –

ALICE. *Connor.*

*(**CONNOR** backs off. **MARNIE** and **ALICE** stare at one another.)*

ALICE. You're –?

(Pause.)

Marnie.

(Pause.)

You're Marnie.

(Pause.)

You're my granddaughter.

(They continue to look at one another.)

Scene Two

(Shortly later. **CONNOR** *stands anxiously near* **MARNIE**, *who sits on the ground, her eyes closed, her mouth moving slightly.)*

*(***CONNOR*** *watches her, unsure of what to do.)*

CONNOR. Well isn't this a surprise, it's –...!

(Pause.)

I haven't seen you since you were seven years old, something like that!

(Pause.)

You remember me?

MARNIE. No.

CONNOR. Oh sure you do, you remember me.

MARNIE. I don't remember you.

CONNOR. Oh! Well.

(Awkward pause.)

Your grandma used to go to the church where my dad was pastor, and once in a while I'd lend a hand to your grandpa out on the feedlot. I babysat for you sometimes when you and your folks lived in that little house on the property over that ridge there, the –...

*(***MARNIE*** *looks at him, not saying anything. Pause.)*

I remember you running down to the river with those crackling balls, you loved those things. You'd run down to the river and light them and then throw them up in the air over the water right before they went off. City council's trying to outlaw those crackling balls, some kid in Troy lit one and dropped it down his shirt or something. They let me have a gun but they wanna take away my crackling balls, it's so –.

(No response.)

You could light a sparkler if you want?

MARNIE. I'm twenty-four years old.

CONNOR. I'm fifty-three and I like sparklers.

> (*Awkward pause.* **MARNIE** *looks at him for a moment, then closes her eyes and continues mouthing something to herself.*)
>
> (**CONNOR** *watches her for a moment.*)

What, um –? What is it that you're – doing?

MARNIE. I'm counting down from one thousand by seven.

> (*Pause.*)

CONNOR. Are you – winning?

MARNIE. It's not a game, it's –. Sometimes it calms me down. What I really want is a cigarette but I'm trying to be healthier about my anxiety.

> (*Pause.*)

CONNOR. Your grandma can be a little prickly, but really she's just a little puppy when it comes down to it, I swear, don't / let her get you –

MARNIE. I'm not worked up because of her, I don't even *know* her.

> (*She looks toward the house, gets up.*)

Okay this is stupid, she can't *hide* from me –

CONNOR. Okay, maybe –. Maybe just give her a minute? I think you caught her a little off-guard.

> (**MARNIE** *stops. Pause. She pulls out a pack of cigarettes, takes one out.*)

Okay if you're gonna light that you need to stand back.

> (*Short pause.*)

MARNIE. Seriously?

CONNOR. One little gust of wind on that cigarette and a piece of ash could fly / right into –

MARNIE. *Okay, okay.*

> (*She gets up, stands away from the fireworks stand, near the plank of particle board. She lights the cigarette, smokes.*)

So you're like – her employee?

(**CONNOR** *looks at her.*)

CONNOR. I'm her roommate and she's lucky I even do anything at this stupid fireworks stand. If it weren't for me working part time at the Walgreens we'd both be on the streets.

(*Pause, brighter:*)

And you're in – Tacoma?

MARNIE. Seattle.

CONNOR. Oh, that's neat! Personally I don't understand the appeal of cities myself, but. I like visiting or whatever, but I couldn't stand living in a little apartment like that, not being able to –

MARNIE. I live on an urban farm.

(*Pause.*)

CONNOR. That's, uh...? I guess I don't know what that is?

MARNIE. I took over a condemned house in the city and turned the property into a farm. We grow vegetables in the front yard, compost in the back. Powered almost entirely by solar, it's getting close to zero impact.

CONNOR. Oh.

(*Pause.*)

That sounds – impressive.

MARNIE. Please don't condescend to me.

CONNOR. I'm not, I / just –

MARNIE. I don't even know you, I don't –...

(**ALICE** *enters, tentatively. She holds a can of soda and a plastic bag.*)

(**MARNIE** *stubs out the cigarette on the particle board, puts the half-smoked cigarette back in the pack.*)

(**ALICE** *looks at* **MARNIE** *for a moment, keeping her distance.*)

(*Pause.*)

ALICE. I brought you, uh –.

> (*She goes to* **MARNIE**, *extending the soda.*)

It's pop, it's –. Diet root beer, it's all we had.

MARNIE. I don't drink soda.

ALICE. Oh.

> (*She pauses, unsure of what to say.* **CONNOR** *keeps his distance.*)
>
> (*She puts the soda down on the cooler.*)
>
> (*Silence.* **CONNOR** *tries to cut the tension.*)

CONNOR. Marnie was just telling me about Seattle.

ALICE. Oh.

CONNOR. She lives on this farm dealie.

ALICE. You live on a *farm*?

MARNIE. Urban farm.

> (*Short pause.* **ALICE** *doesn't understand.*)

ALICE. Okay.

> (*Pause.*)

Connor, could you –?

> (**CONNOR** *exits toward the house.* **ALICE** *and* **MARNIE** *stand for a moment in silence, looking at one another.*)

You really walked all the way here from town?

> (*Pause.*)

How did you get to Lewiston?

MARNIE. Took a bus.

ALICE. It was okay?

MARNIE. No. I had to transfer in Spokane, waited at the station for six hours. A guy named "Buffalo" offered me an Altoid, it was horrifying.

> (*Pause.*)

You *really* didn't recognize me?

ALICE. It's been quite a while, I –.

> *(Pause.)*

You hungry at all?

> *(She reaches into the plastic bag, pulls out a Ziploc bag with some jerky inside.)*

MARNIE. What is it?

ALICE. Elk jerky. Connor shot an elk last season and the idiot doesn't even *like* elk so I've been eating this stupid elk jerky for months.

MARNIE. I don't eat meat.

ALICE. When did that happen?

MARNIE. A long time ago.

ALICE. That's so sad.

> *(She reaches into the bag, pulls out a small bag of carrot sticks.)*

They're a couple weeks old, not looking too good. Have 'em.

> *(Pause. **MARNIE** takes the carrots, eats one. She keeps her distance from **ALICE**.)*

So you –... I thought you were in Tacoma, you live on a farm, or –?

MARNIE. Urban farm. It's a business I started, a sustainable agricultural project in the city. But I left a few days ago.

ALICE. Why?

MARNIE. Because I realized that I was surrounded by fucking assholes.

ALICE. Well I don't need to hear that / language, but –

MARNIE. I started it five years ago with a *very* specific mission, and bit by bit everyone who's come on board has managed to chip away at it, and –. It just – got out of control.

ALICE. Okay.

> *(Short pause.)*

ALICE. And how were you able to start something like that?

MARNIE. I dropped out of college, used the rest of the money Mom left me to start it.

    (Pause.)

ALICE. You –? And your father was okay with that?

MARNIE. I don't really talk to him anymore.

    (Pause.)

ALICE. I didn't know that.

MARNIE. Well you haven't exactly made an effort to keep in touch, have you?

    (She takes out her cigarettes, taking out the partially-smoked one from before.)

ALICE. When did that start up?

MARNIE. *Now* you're being parental?

ALICE. I'm not your parent. Gimme one.

    *(**MARNIE** gives **ALICE** a cigarette, hands her a lighter.)*

Connor made me quit a few years ago when I fell asleep at the stand, when I woke up I had dropped a cigarette on a cardboard box and was about two seconds away from the biggest fireworks display this town has ever seen. So I quit, mostly.

    *(**MARNIE** lights her cigarette, smokes.)*

MARNIE. Connor is –?

ALICE. He's my roommate.

MARNIE. Oh.

ALICE. We're not involved.

MARNIE. Obviously.

ALICE. What's that supposed to mean? He's not *that* much younger than me.

MARNIE. That's *not* what I was talking about.

    (Pause.)

ALICE. Marnie, I know that I haven't been a part of your life for quite some time, but I want you to know that I'm not a terrible person, I'm / not –

MARNIE. I don't know *anything* about you, I don't *want* to know anything about you. Honestly the only thing I *really* remember is that I hated it when my parents were both away because that meant I had to stay in your house.

ALICE. Oh that's bull, you loved staying there.

MARNIE. No, / I didn't –

ALICE. The second bedroom had a waterbed, you loved it.

(*Short pause.*)

That's really all you remember?

(*Pause.*)

MARNIE. I mean I remember Mom, is that what you're talking / about?

ALICE. *No*, that's not –. That's not what I'm talking about.

(*Silence. She looks away.*)

I can see if there's more food in the house, I don't have much in the way of vegetarian entrees, but I'm sure we / could –

MARNIE. How much land do you have left?

(*Pause.* **ALICE** *looks at her.*)

ALICE. I mean not a lot, it's just twenty acres or so –

MARNIE. I'll give you thirty thousand for it.

(*Pause.*)

Given that this land was supposed to be mine anyway, I think that's totally reasonable.

(*Pause.*)

ALICE. What are you / saying, what –?

MARNIE. You can use it to buy someplace in town, or rent or whatever, just please pick someplace far away from here so we don't have to –

ALICE. *Marnie.*

>   *(Pause.)*

MARNIE. Look, I didn't just *leave* the urban farm, I was *bought* out. And if I'd known that you had been selling the land like this I –. I'm not letting you sell off this last piece of it. This place has been in our family for six generations and I'm not letting you screw it up for the next six.

>   *(Pause.)*

ALICE. Marnie, this –. Whether you like it or not, this land is still mine, and I can sell it to whoever I / see fit –

MARNIE. You know when I was a little girl, this place meant something to you, you would / tell me –

ALICE. That was a long time ago, Marnie, and I don't –... Alright I just can't stand this conversation anymore, I think I'm done.

>   *(She sits down on her lawn chair, opens the cooler.)*

Dammit Connor did you / drink *everything*?

MARNIE. If I need to get a lawyer involved, then I will.

>   *(**CONNOR** appears in the back with a plate of tater tots; he stops when he senses the tension.)*

ALICE. I'm so sick of that man drinking / all of my beer –

MARNIE. Are you even fucking *listening* to me?!

ALICE. STOP USING THAT WORD.

CONNOR. Hey you two.

>   *(**ALICE** and **MARNIE** both look at **CONNOR**. Pause.)*

I overheard you saying that you were a vegetarian, so I microwaved the leftover tots from last night.

>   *(Pause. **ALICE** and **MARNIE** take a breath.)*

MARNIE. Thank you.

> (**CONNOR** *takes the tray down to* **MARNIE** *and* **ALICE**. **ALICE** *pops one in her mouth,* **MARNIE** *takes a few in her hand.*)

Thank you, I'm actually starving.

CONNOR. Oh now I did grease the pan last night with elk fat, just so you know.

ALICE. Jesus, Connor.

> (**MARNIE** *puts the tots back on the plate.*)

CONNOR. I'm *sorry*, we've got a lot of elk fat! We have to use it on / something!

ALICE. Never mind, thank you, Connor, thank you.

> (*Awkward silence.* **MARNIE** *looks out toward the river.*)

MARNIE. (*Pointing.*) We used to go hiking up there.

ALICE. What?

MARNIE. Up there. The ridge up there, I remember hiking it with you and Mom.

> (**ALICE** *looks.*)

ALICE. Oh.

MARNIE. You remember that?

ALICE. Yeah, I –. I guess I do.

> (*Pause.*)

MARNIE. You would look over the ranch, and you'd tell us that we were a part of the town's history. That you and me and Mom had a responsibility to this place. That you could draw a direct line from your great-grandpa, a hundred and fifty years ago, to the three of us, right at that second.

> (*Pause.*)

Guess you fucked that up, huh?

> (*Pause.* **ALICE** *goes to the cashbox, counting out some cash.*)

ALICE. I think – you should just go home, Marnie. I'm going to give you some cash for a taxi, there are a few more buses that leave to Spokane today.

MARNIE. I don't think you understand, I'm not going anywhere.

ALICE. I am not in a position to have another houseguest right now, so just take the money, and call a cab –

> (**MARNIE** *takes off her backpack, opening it up. She takes out a small tent, starts setting it up.*)

Oh for God's sake, Marnie, you can't camp here –

MARNIE. Well then I guess you'll have to call the police.

ALICE. / Don't test me, Marnie!

CONNOR. Okay, okay, just –!

> (*Silence.* **MARNIE** *and* **ALICE** *calm down.*)

How about this, why don't I –? I'll make a run into town, get us all something to eat.

> (*No response.*)

Okay then! Alice, I can take the pickup?

> (*Pause.* **ALICE** *reaches into her pocket, hands her keys to* **CONNOR**.)

ALICE. Don't wreck it.

CONNOR. I'm not gonna *wreck* it, god.

ALICE. You're awful with a stick shift, don't wreck it.

> (**CONNOR** *starts to exit, then turns to them.*)

CONNOR. I think it's really nice, seeing you two together again.

> (*Pause.*)

I just wanted to say that.

> (*He exits.*)

> (*A very long silence between* **MARNIE** *and* **ALICE** *as* **MARNIE** *continues to set up the tent.* **ALICE** *watches her.*)

(Finally:)

ALICE. Do you want / me to [help you] –?

MARNIE. *(Sharp.)* I'm fine.

> *(She finishes pitching the tent, then looks at* **ALICE**. *A silence as they stare at one another.)*

> *(Finally,* **MARNIE** *goes into the tent, closing the front flap. Pause.)*

ALICE. It'll get pretty hot if you don't open the flaps, Marnie. You'll bake like a casserole.

> *(Pause. A small flap opens on the side of the tent.)*

> *(Silence.* **ALICE** *turns to leave.)*

MARNIE. You could have called.

> *(Pause.)*

You could have done something.

> *(***ALICE** *is about to say something, stops herself.)*

> *(Silence.)*

Hello?

> *(Pause.* **ALICE** *gets up, heading back up toward the house. She exits.)*

> *(Another pause.)*

> *(***MARNIE** *unzips the front of the tent, pokes her head out. She looks toward* **ALICE**, *sees that she's gone.)*

Darkness

(As before, we hear the sounds of wind through trees, birds, this time accompanied by the steady rhythm of footsteps falling on ground covered with leaves and sticks.)

FEMALE VOICE. So I don't know if I –…? I'm getting close to Great Falls, I know that much, but I'm not exactly sure where I –…

(Pause.)

I can't believe I've never been here before. This is probably only a seven- or eight-hour drive from Lewiston, how have I never –…? And it's just so – *huge*, it feels like this landscape could go on forever. I've been up since three in the morning, walking for – fifteen, sixteen hours, and I feel like I could keep going for another sixteen, I –

(Pause. The footsteps stop.)

Oh, wow, I can –…

(Pause. Some rustling, a few more footsteps. A small laugh.)

I can see two separate thunderstorms, I can see one in the distance in front of me, and in back of me there's another one coming over the mountains.

(Pause.)

Huh.

(Pause.)

It's interesting, walking the trail like this, it's making me realize – this must have been *terrifying* for Lewis and Clark. Leading dozens of people across the country, and you never know what's going to happen next, you have no idea if –… That's the thing you always forget when you read about them, they were still just – people.

(As the voice continues, lights slowly rise on:)

Scene Three

(A few hours later, getting dark. The stage is bare.)

(From inside the tent, we hear the **FEMALE VOICE** *coming from a small tape player.)*

*(**CONNOR** enters, carrying two pizzas. He approaches Marnie's tent slowly.)*

FEMALE VOICE. It's so simple, it's not –. I mean it sounds almost dumb to say it, but I've been reading about Meriwether Lewis my entire life, but now that I'm actually here, it's reminding me that he was / an *actual person*, he was –

CONNOR. *(Softly.)* ...Marnie?

*(A small scream from inside the tent, **MARNIE** thrashes a bit. The tape player stops.)*

Sorry sorry sorry it's me!

*(**MARNIE** finally manages to unzip the tent; she looks at **CONNOR**.)*

I got pizza?

(Short pause.)

One of them's called a "Garden Veggie." Broccoli and stuff, it looks awful, you'll love it.

*(**MARNIE** comes out of the tent.)*

Sorry about that.

MARNIE. It's fine, just –. Thank you, I'm starving, thank you.

(She opens up the pizza box, takes a piece of pizza out, and starts eating.)

How much do I owe you?

CONNOR. Oh don't worry about it, it's not –

*(**MARNIE** reaches into her pocket, taking out some cash.)*

MARNIE. No, really, how / much –

CONNOR. I won't hear of it. Honestly.

> (**MARNIE** *relents, puts the money back in her pocket.*)

MARNIE. Thank you.

> (*Her cell phone vibrates. She takes it out of her pocket, looks at it.*)

CONNOR. (*Motioning toward the house.*) I can, uh –

MARNIE. No, it's fine.

> (*She silences her phone, puts it back in her pocket.*)

> (**CONNOR** *opens up the other pizza; it's covered in various types of meat.* **MARNIE** *looks at it.*)

God, what is that?

CONNOR. What? It's a meat lover's. What?

MARNIE. How many different kinds of animals are on that?

CONNOR. Two. Well no three.

> (**MARNIE** *recoils.*)

Oh please. Honey, I seem to remember that when you were a little girl your favorite food was hot dogs, so.

MARNIE. That is *not true.*

CONNOR. Oh really?

MARNIE. I ate meat when I was a kid because I didn't know better. I hated that we raised cattle, I thought it was awful.

CONNOR. Oh that's a load of bull. When you were a little kid you used to name the pigs in the summer and eat 'em in the winter, you loved it.

MARNIE. I named them because I felt *bad* for them –

CONNOR. Oh is that why?

MARNIE. *Yes.*

CONNOR. So you felt real bad for the pig you named "Spam"?

> (*Short pause.*)

MARNIE. I – did *not* name one that –

(**CONNOR** *gets up, taking his pizza.*)

CONNOR. Well anyway if my delicious dead animals are that offensive, I can just –

MARNIE. Wait, just –...

(*Pause.*)

I need someone to make her listen to reason.

(*Pause.*)

CONNOR. Okay?

MARNIE. I don't know what kind of – arrangement you guys have going here. But I had no idea that she was selling off the land like this, and I have a chance to save this one little part of it, and I –... I'm offering her a very decent price for it.

(*Pause.*)

CONNOR. Wait, you wanna *buy the land* from her?

(*Pause.*)

You have money?

MARNIE. Yeah, I have money.

(*Pause.*)

CONNOR. You don't have money.

MARNIE. Yes, I do.

CONNOR. Bullcrap you're like seventeen, you don't have money.

MARNIE. I am *twenty-four* and I started one of the most successful environmental projects Seattle's seen in *years*, so yes, I have money. I want her to take thirty thousand for what's left of the land. And I think that's *totally reasonable*.

CONNOR. You have thirty thousand dollars?

MARNIE. Yes.

CONNOR. Your pizza cost twelve bucks.

> *(Pause.* **MARNIE** *reaches into her pocket, gives him cash.)*

CONNOR. You know, she's already been talking to the Meriwether Terrace people, they're offering her a lot more than thirty thousand, and a two-bedroom by the pool –

MARNIE. I realize she doesn't give a crap about this place, or her family for that matter –

CONNOR. Now your grandma loves you, I know that for certain, don't –

> *(***MARNIE***'s phone vibrates again. She angrily takes it out of her pocket, silences it.)*

MARNIE. *Fucking stop, James.*

> *(She throws the phone in her tent. Pause.)*

CONNOR. Okay – you gotta understand, this has been in the works for a *while* now. And to be honest I've been looking forward to that condo for quite some time now, and –

MARNIE. Whatever, forget it, I didn't realize she was your *meal ticket* or whatever.

> *(Pause.)*

CONNOR. I'm sorry, *what*?

MARNIE. Never mind.

CONNOR. That woman is *not* my meal ticket, if anything I am *her* sugar daddy, and – I mean not like *that*, I – anyway, *I'm* the one with a paying job, I'm the one who actually gets a paycheck and pays the bills and buys the groceries.

MARNIE. Okay, you're her sugar daddy then, fine.

CONNOR. Okay let's just both stop using that phrase, okay?

MARNIE. No, I'm sure your job at "the Walgreens" brings in plenty of cash, I'm very impressed.

> *(Short pause.* **CONNOR** *looks at her.)*

CONNOR. You've turned into quite the little brat over the years, huh?

MARNIE. Forget it. Thank you for the pizza, Connor, thank you / for –

CONNOR. Four years ago, she got skin cancer. Did you know that?

(Pause.)

Did you?

MARNIE. No, I didn't / know that –

CONNOR. When she got the diagnosis, I started working overtime to help her with the hospital bills, went with her to *every* chemo treatment, didn't leave her side for a year and a half. She got through that whole ordeal cancer- *and* debt-free.

(Pause.)

And I had a career once, a *good* career. When I got laid off, the only place in town I could find work was the Walgreens, and believe me, I'm not happy about it.

(Pause.)

MARNIE. I'm sorry.

CONNOR. Mm-hm.

MARNIE. *I'm sorry.* I was being mean. I was being mean *and* classist.

(Pause.)

Things in my life are sort of up in the air right now, and I guess I've become an asshole without even noticing.

*(Silence. **CONNOR** sits down, eating his pizza.)*

What kind of job did you have?

CONNOR. I was in processing.

MARNIE. Huh. That's like –. I mean that's like an office job, or –?

CONNOR. No, no, *meat* processing, I was a butcher. I was with J&L over in Clarkston for seventeen years before they shut down. Great place, family run.

MARNIE. You're a butcher?

CONNOR. I was trained in taxidermy at first. But art doesn't pay the bills, so.

(**MARNIE** *looks away.*)

CONNOR. What?

MARNIE. Nothing, it's –. Nothing.

CONNOR. Oh here we go.

MARNIE. Sorry, I just don't see how you could have devoted your *life* to something like that.

CONNOR. Well excuse me for participating in the food chain.

MARNIE. And what does *taxidermy* have to / do with the food chain?

CONNOR. I said I *used* to be a taxidermist. And you realize people still eat the meat when something gets mounted, I just took the skin / and put it on a form.

MARNIE. Okay please stop describing it.

CONNOR. Oh well lah dee dah, look who's too good for the food chain.

MARNIE. I'm not "too good" for it, I just think that there's a way to live your life where you don't have to kill other animals just to survive, there's a / way to –

CONNOR. Oh please educate me, please save this country rube.

MARNIE. I'm just saying, there are other ways to get protein other / than –

CONNOR. And good for you, you can saunter on down to the organic grocery store and buy your organic almonds and tofu and whatever else, you think your ancestors who homesteaded here in eighteen-whatever could hop on down to the food co-op when they were hungry? Whether you like it or not, you come from a proud line of *cattle ranchers*. Your ancestors ate meat just like their ancestors did, so you can pretend to be a vegetarian all you want but it's been part of your DNA for thousands of years.

MARNIE. Yeah, well, we also descended from apes, does that mean I should be naked and throwing my own feces?

CONNOR. Oh you're one of those as well then.

(**ALICE** *appears in the back.* **CONNOR** *and* **MARNIE** *don't notice her.*)

MARNIE. Wait, what?

CONNOR. Oh no, I'm not getting / into this one.

MARNIE. *Evolution*, is that what you're talking about? You can't be serious, you don't believe in *evolution*?

CONNOR. I said I am *not* getting into / this –

MARNIE. What *are* you?!

CONNOR. I am allowed / to believe whatever I want –

MARNIE. I can't believe that someone who thinks that the earth is like five thousand years old is lecturing me about *history*. You believe that cavemen like, *rode dinosaurs* –

CONNOR. Oh yes, that's right, that's what I believe. Thank you.

(**ALICE** *makes her way to a box, opens it up. She rummages around in it a bit.*)

Listen let's just say, I'm allowed to eat animals like people have been doing for thousands of years, and you're allowed to believe that human life is one big random accident.

MARNIE. So you think that we just all like, *appeared* here, on this planet, along with every other species on Earth –?

(**ALICE** *takes a small firework out of the box, takes a lighter out of her pocket, lights the firework, drops it into an empty bucket.*)

CONNOR. I *believe* that our existence on Earth was guided by God, that we are here for a *reason* and that the natural beauty of the world was made by an intelligent force, and wasn't just some random, meaningless –

(*The firework explodes with a very loud bang.* **MARNIE** *lets out a little scream,* **CONNOR** *ducks and covers.*)

(*Pause.* **CONNOR** *looks at* **ALICE.**)

CONNOR. Where'd you get that?

ALICE. I've had these M-80s sitting around since the early nineties. Back from when we could actually sell the *good* fireworks.

CONNOR. You're lucky a cop car wasn't rolling by on the highway just then.

ALICE. Oh let 'em arrest me, I don't care.

MARNIE. That was *really mean.*

ALICE. Well.

MARNIE. I thought I was being *shot* at.

ALICE. Oo, meat lover's.

> *(She goes to the pizza, taking a slice.)*
>
> *(**MARNIE** goes into her tent, zips up the door. The zipper gets caught midway; she tugs at it.)*

Slow, Marnie.

> *(**MARNIE** seethes, zipping it up slower. She closes the flap. Pause. **ALICE** and **CONNOR** eat their pizza.)*

The Meriwether Terrace people called me just now.

> *(Pause.)*

CONNOR. Again?

ALICE. They said they're anxious to get going, break ground.

CONNOR. Why're they calling this late?

ALICE. How should I know?

> *(Short pause.)*

CONNOR. Did they – make a new offer?

ALICE. Oh don't worry about it.

CONNOR. What? We agreed, I'm better at this stuff than you are –

ALICE. Oh shut up, I'm just fine at it.

CONNOR. Oh yeah? Ken Donnelly got you to sell him that riding lawn mower for two hundred bucks last year –

ALICE. Shut up I said! That thing wasn't worth more than two hundred –

CONNOR. That "thing" was a John Deere, I paid nine-fifty for that thing two years before you went and sold it / behind my back –

ALICE. Anyway it's *done*, I said yes to the offer. I said they can send me the contracts and I'll sign.

> *(Pause.* **MARNIE** *opens the tent, coming outside.)*

CONNOR. You –? You took it?

> *(Pause.* **ALICE** *starts walking around the shelves, looking at the fireworks.)*

ALICE. I just felt like it was time. No use drawing this out any longer than we need to.

CONNOR. Alice, I thought we were gonna wait a couple weeks, see if they upped the offer –

ALICE. Oh the offer was fine. Anyway it's done, it's my decision and I took it.

MARNIE. Wait, you –? You're just selling it, just like that?

> *(***ALICE** *picks up a firework.)*

CONNOR. Ally, I know it's your decision, but I thought we agreed that I should be the one talking to Brad –

ALICE. Well I changed my mind! I just gave Brent – *his name is Brent* – a call and told him I'm ready to take the deal.
(Re: the firework.) These aren't twelve ninety-five, you labeled them wrong.

CONNOR. You called *him*? I just don't understand, I thought we were working together on this, why would you do this behind my back?

> *(***MARNIE** *goes to* **ALICE**.*)*

MARNIE. Okay, you can't do this –

ALICE. Actually I *can* do this, Marnie, it's my land and I can do whatever the hell I want with it!

(She goes back to the fireworks.)

ALICE. Where are the damn tags? You labeled this wrong, it's nine ninety-five, not twelve ninety-five.

CONNOR. I did *not* label them wrong, the Grand Pagodas are twelve ninety-five.

ALICE. No, they're nine ninety-five.

CONNOR. I explained this to you, the distributor marked up the prices a dollar this year –

ALICE. You're thinking of the Happy American Rainbow Wheel. Where's the marker?

CONNOR. No, I'm not! I actually *know* what they cost because I'm the only one who even tries to keep track of our inventory!

ALICE. Well if you don't do a decent job of it, then what good is it at all?!

MARNIE. Hello?!

*(**ALICE** grabs a marker off the table.)*

ALICE. I'm changing the damn tag.

*(**CONNOR** tries to take the marker from her.)*

CONNOR. Gimme that marker.

ALICE. / It's my marker!

MARNIE. I *will* get a lawyer involved then / I will –

ALICE. ALRIGHT ENOUGH.

(Pause.)

Marnie – you can just pack up your things and leave, right now. It's done. I know you had some idea about taking over this place, but that is *never going to happen.* I've sold it, it's done.

(Pause.)

Okay?

*(Silence. **MARNIE** glares at her.)*

MARNIE. I had a pretty fucking low opinion of you before today, I didn't think it could go much lower.

*(Pause. **ALICE** looks away.)*

ALICE. Believe what you want, Marnie.

MARNIE. You know, I remember some other stuff about living here when I was a kid. I remember the fights, I remember you lecturing Mom about responsibility and adulthood, I remember you making her feel like she was *nothing.*

CONNOR. / Okay, guys –

ALICE. I'm tired of this conversation, / Marnie, I really am –

MARNIE. I remember when she got back from walking the Lewis and Clark Trail, I remember waking up the next morning and there was an ambulance parked down by the river, and I was confused why Mom was in the water face down –

ALICE. *(Exploding.)* JUST GO HOME, MARNIE, JUST –

(She stops herself, struggling to calm down.)

(Silence.)

Pack up your stuff and go. If you're still here in the morning, I'll call the police.

CONNOR. Alice –

ALICE. This is my house, this is my land, and I don't care what either of you think.

*(She heads back up to the house. **CONNOR** watches her go.)*

(Silence.)

CONNOR. Well. Thanks for that. If we would have held out a little longer we probably could have gotten one of the three bedrooms, or a *Jacuzzi suite*, or –...

(Pause.)

Get your stuff together, I'll drive you back to the bus station.

MARNIE. I'm not leaving.

*(Short pause. **CONNOR** looks at her.)*

CONNOR. Honey.

MARNIE. I'm serious, there's no way I'm letting her do this.

CONNOR. Oh for God's sake, how much chaos can one person create in a single day?! You lost, Marnie, time to go home –

MARNIE. This place is mine as much as it is hers, I'm not going anywhere –

CONNOR. Oh you're just entitled to it, is that it?! You haven't set foot here in fifteen years, and now you think you can just waltz on in here and take over the place?

MARNIE. You have no idea who I am or what I've been through, this is a lot more complicated than you realize –

CONNOR. Oh because I'd never understand someone as deep and profound as you, is that it?! You know, you can pretend to be the enlightened, educated adult all you want, but underneath it all you're obviously just a *frightened little child.*

MARNIE. *Yeah well you're obviously some closeted gay guy who can't even deal with –...!*

(*Pause.* **CONNOR** *stares at her.*)

I'm sorry, I don't mean –...

(*Short pause.*)

Look I shouldn't have said that, your personal life is –... But I'm just saying, it's *totally unfair* that you're, like, talking down to me when you can't even deal with the *basics* of your own personality –

CONNOR. How simple do you think I am?

(*Pause.*)

You are a person who lives *entirely* for herself, you know that? You expect everything in the world to conform around *you*, to bend to suit *your* needs and *your* personality, and the moment that it stops conforming – you melt down. I have lived my life bending to the will of the world around me, that's the difference between you and me. Growing up in this town, a minister for a father *and* a brother, I –...

(*Silence.* **CONNOR** *looks away.*)

MARNIE. But don't you want to – I don't know, self-actualize or whatever?

CONNOR. Seems like you've been self-actualizing your entire life, how's that going for you?

(Pause.)

MARNIE. I'm sorry, I –...

(Pause.)

I'm just sorry.

*(Pause. **CONNOR** relents, taking a breath.)*

You know, I – actually do remember you. From when I was little.

(Pause.)

CONNOR. You do?

MARNIE. Yeah. I mean you were a lot younger back then.

CONNOR. Yes, thank you for that.

MARNIE. Did you and my grandma take me to a fair with like – farm equipment, and –?

CONNOR. The tractor pull? I can't believe you remember that, you couldn't have been four years old. Your grandma and I babysat you quite a bit back then.

MARNIE. Why?

(Pause.)

CONNOR. I mean – your mom had good periods and bad periods, Marnie. And your grandma and I would – help out.

*(Silence. **MARNIE** thinks.)*

MARNIE. I have these memories of her. My grandma, I mean. And they're actually – *nice*. It doesn't make sense.

(Pause.)

CONNOR. She *does* care about you, Marnie –

MARNIE. Caring for someone means actually *showing* that you care for them. It means *demonstrating* care for another person, not cutting them out of your life completely. I mean my dad wasn't much of a help in my life, either. But at least he put a roof over my head until I was eighteen, didn't touch the money Mom left me.

(Pause.)

CONNOR. Marnie, you can't actually –... Think this through. What are you gonna do with twenty acres pushed up against some ugly condos?

MARNIE. I don't know. Raise a family?

(Pause.)

When I got to Lewiston earlier, I started walking down the highway, and I was so – lost. I had no idea where I was heading, I thought I remembered which direction the ranch was, but it didn't look right, nothing was familiar. And finally I went into a gas station to get some water, and as I was paying I looked out the window and I saw this tree that was like twenty or so feet away, and suddenly I realized – that tree was outside my bedroom window. I used to climb that tree, I fell out of that tree once and sprained my wrist. The gas station is exactly where our house was. And the feeling was so weird, it was like – remembering how happy I had been here once, but now, I'm back, and I feel so –...

(Silence. **CONNOR** *looks at* **MARNIE**.*)*

CONNOR. Talk with your grandma, Marnie. I'm not –.

(Pause.)

I'm not family.

(Pause. He looks toward the river, lost in thought. **MARNIE** *watches him.)*

I think I'm gonna go for a drive. Have whatever you want out of the cooler.

*(***MARNIE** *watches him go. We hear the sound of the pickup starting up and driving away.)*

Darkness

(As before, we begin to hear the sounds of wind rustling through trees, birds, etc., accompanied by the steady rhythm of footsteps.)

FEMALE VOICE. It was at least three or four of the cubs, and I realized, I was *in between* them. And that's *bad*, being in between a mother and her cubs? That's when a black bear could attack, but I –

(We hear some rustling, the recording distorts momentarily.)

(Laughing.) Okay! I almost sprained my ankle there, which would have been *bad*, so... Pay more attention, Catherine...

(Short pause.)

Anyway I saw this mother bear and for some reason I just knew – it was fine. And she looked at me for a second or two, and I swear – this is so stupid, I know, I hear how stupid this sounds – but it was like I somehow let her know that I wasn't a threat. And she understood, and she just – left. With her cubs following behind her.

(The footsteps stop. We hear a long breath. Lights rise on:)

Scene Four

(The next day, late morning.)

*(****MARNIE*** *is looking through the fireworks, listening to the tape player.)*

FEMALE VOICE. I mean I know it's silly, but it's almost like –

*(****ALICE*** *enters, dressed in funeral black.* ***MARNIE*** *doesn't see her at first.)*

I feel this sense of – of connection, of forward movement.

*(****ALICE***, *recognizing the recording, stops.)*

(A pause on the tape. We hear a breath.)

It's like there's this constant potential for / something *new* to present itself to you, something –

ALICE. Where did you get that?

*(****MARNIE*** *turns, sees* ***ALICE***. *She turns the tape off.)*

MARNIE. My dad.

(Pause.)

ALICE. You've listened to them before?

MARNIE. No, I –.

(Pause.)

ALICE. You shouldn't be listening to those, it's pointless to dig up all this, / you –

MARNIE. Why?

(Silence. ***ALICE*** *looks away.)*

ALICE. Is Connor –...?

MARNIE. He's not here.

(Pause.)

I thought you were going to call the cops, have me removed.

ALICE. I still might.

(Pause.)

You have breakfast?

MARNIE. There was leftover pizza.

ALICE. For breakfast?

MARNIE. It's fine.

(Pause.)

What's with [the clothes] –?

ALICE. Oh, I –. Funeral.

MARNIE. Oh.

(Pause.)

Was it –? Someone close, or –?

ALICE. Not especially. I mean it hit me in a certain way, but nothing too devastating. It gets easier as you get older, anyway, death starts to mean less and less. I remember when I was a little girl, my horse died and I thought the world was caving in on me.

*(**MARNIE** continues looking through the fireworks. Pause.)*

MARNIE. Which are the ones, the like tubes that shoot the flaming balls?

ALICE. Roman candles, we can't sell those.

MARNIE. What about the bees, the bee things?

ALICE. Illegal.

MARNIE. *Those stupid little things?!*

ALICE. Anything that goes up into the air. It's not "safe and sane," that's what they call them.

MARNIE. What does that leave?

ALICE. Fountains, sparklers, smoke bombs, little rolly things. Not much else.

MARNIE. That sucks.

ALICE. Yeah, it does.

(Pause.)

I'm surprised you remember all these things.

MARNIE. Yeah, me too. I mean, Mom loved them, we'd light them off together all the time, we –.

> *(She stops herself. Pause. She goes back to the fireworks, picks one up.)*

What does this one do?

ALICE. I don't know, read the thing.

MARNIE. *(Reading the tag.)* "Behold a cataclysmic –"

ALICE. Never mind. Dammit, Connor. It's just a stupid little fountain. Most of them do the same thing, anyway, they just have different names.

> **(MARNIE** *puts the firework back. Pause.)*

MARNIE. Who was it who [died]...?

ALICE. Oh, Scotty, was his name. My nephew Scotty.

> *(Pause.)*

MARNIE. Wait, *Scott*? Mom's cousin?

ALICE. Yeah, that's him.

MARNIE. He *died*?

ALICE. He certainly did.

MARNIE. That's –.

> *(Pause.)*

I remember Scott, I was the flower girl at his wedding –

ALICE. Oh, that marriage lasted all of twenty / minutes –

MARNIE. *He died?*

> *(Pause.* **ALICE** *looks at her.)*

ALICE. Yes, Marnie, he died, he's dead. It was awful, too, a real mess, drove up the grade on the wrong side of the road and plowed straight into a gravel truck.

MARNIE. Jesus.

ALICE. He was a nice kid, but he'd been struggling with drugs for years so it's unfortunately not altogether / surprising –

MARNIE. You didn't think to *tell* me?

ALICE. I honestly didn't think you'd even remember who the man was. I'm sorry.

> *(Pause.* **MARNIE** *picks up another firework, looking at it.)*

MARNIE. "Lady Liberty Cone."

ALICE. Oh yeah, I remember that one, Connor set one off the other night.

MARNIE. Is it good?

ALICE. Not bad. Red and blue I think, four or five feet tall, lasts a couple seconds.

MARNIE. A *couple seconds*?

ALICE. It costs eighty-five cents, what do you want?

> *(Pause.* **MARNIE** *goes back to the fireworks.* **ALICE** *tentatively sits down.)*

So – you ended up leaving college pretty quick.

MARNIE. If this is going to turn into a lecture, I / don't need to –

ALICE. I'm not, I'm –.

> *(***MARNIE** *looks at her for a moment, then goes back to the fireworks.)*

MARNIE. I left like halfway through my first semester.

> *(Pause.)*

ALICE. Were you failing, / or –?

MARNIE. *No*, I –. The freshman classes were a joke, I could have taken those tests *high* and still passed everything. I just –.

> *(Pause.)*

ALICE. What did you study?

MARNIE. History.

> *(Short pause.)*

I guess after a while I just sort of looked at what I was doing and realized I didn't have any faith in it.

ALICE. Why didn't / you have –?

MARNIE. I mean you spend long enough thinking about everything that came before you and after a while it just reveals itself to be a random string of events with no real *purpose*, no *causality* other than death motivated by greed and random coincidence.

>   *(Pause.)*

I know that sounds cynical.

ALICE. It just sounds like you're in your early twenties.

>   (**MARNIE** *continues to look through the fireworks. Pause.*)

MARNIE. What's this one do?

ALICE. It's a smoke bomb. Makes smoke.

MARNIE. Boring.

>   *(Pause. She continues to look.)*

ALICE. So your dad, he –...

>   *(Pause.)*

You two don't get on so well now?

MARNIE. It's whatever. I don't care.

>   *(Pause.)*

After Dad and I moved to Tacoma, after Mom died, he started drinking more. A lot more.

>   *(Pause.)*

ALICE. Oh.

>   (**MARNIE** *grabs a firework. Pause.*)

MARNIE. What about this one?

ALICE. What's it called?

MARNIE. "Golden Shower." Heh.

ALICE. What?

MARNIE. Nothing. What's it do?

ALICE. I would imagine it's along the lines of a shower that is golden. Light the thing if you want.

(**MARNIE** *goes to the particle board, puts the fountain on it. Pause.*)

Did your dad ever –? He didn't have a temper, did he?

MARNIE. He wasn't abusive, if that's what you're asking. He was just – pathetic.

(*She moves to the particle board, puts the firework on top of it. She pulls out a lighter, standing back, carefully moving the flame toward the firework.*)

ALICE. Just light it.

MARNIE. I am.

ALICE. It won't explode in your face, just light it.

MARNIE. I'm just [being careful] –.

(*She is about to light the firework, then stops herself, looking at it. The flame on the lighter goes out.*)

(*She stares at the firework, not saying anything. Silence.*)

ALICE. Marnie, / are you –?

MARNIE. You know I always thought you blamed me.

(*Pause.*)

ALICE. For what?

MARNIE. Mom killing herself.

(*She looks at* **ALICE**. *Silence.*)

ALICE. Marnie, I / never –

MARNIE. Well Mom drowned herself in the river, suddenly we lived in this new city, and I never heard from you *ever*, you just became this *ghost* in my life, and I –... I was eight years old, what the hell was I supposed to think?

(*The sound of a car driving up, parking.* **ALICE** *and* **MARNIE** *look away from one another.*)

(**CONNOR** *enters.*)

ALICE. Where the hell have you been?!

CONNOR. I drove up to the top of the bluff, that lookout over the valley. Ended up falling asleep in the pickup.

ALICE. You were supposed to take me to Scotty's funeral, I had to get a ride with Janice.

CONNOR. Janice –?

ALICE. His ex-wife, the crazy person! She tried to hug me, it was awful!

CONNOR. I'm sorry, Alice, I didn't mean to fall asleep.

> (**ALICE** *busies herself with straightening up fireworks.*)

Listen, I –. I did some thinking when I was up there.

ALICE. I really could have used some company at that funeral, you know?

CONNOR. I barely knew Scott, you know that.

ALICE. Well you told me you would come, I had to go by myself which was very unpleasant.

CONNOR. Well, I'm sorry, but –

ALICE. There were only three other people there, I had no idea who they even were. They had this preacher from the Unitarian church say a few things, these damn Unitarians, I never understand a word / they say –

CONNOR. Alice.

ALICE. The least you could have done was run the stand while I was gone, Henry Womer told me last week he would come by today to pick up a couple variety packs, so for all we know we've lost that business –

CONNOR. I put my name in for a job in Pocatello this morning.

> (**ALICE** *stops, looks at him.*)

ALICE. You –? What?

CONNOR. Little place that makes sausage mostly, game processing on the side. They're looking for a full-time butcher. Randy from J&L works there now, he's gonna put in a good word.

*(Pause. **ALICE** goes to the cooler.)*

ALICE. Oh shut up, Connor.

CONNOR. You think I'm lying? It's called Henderson Lockers, you can look it up. They've got six full-time butchers, looking for a seventh.

ALICE. You told me you were picking up more beer –

CONNOR. I did, it's in there.

ALICE. You got *Coors*? I can't drink this!

CONNOR. *Alice.*

*(**ALICE** stops, looks at him.)*

ALICE. Fine, Connor, you want my attention, you got it, you –…

(Pause. She looks at him, finally accepting that he's being serious.)

Pocatello? You wanna move to *Pocatello?*

(Pause.)

CONNOR. I thought a lot about this, and I just think – maybe it's time for me to move on. You're gonna be moving into a new place, you're not gonna wanna have me hanging around your neck for the rest of your life. This wasn't permanent, we both knew that, we –…

(Pause.)

And, honestly, maybe – it'd be best for both of us.

*(Pause. **ALICE** looks at him for a moment, then starts to head for the house.)*

Alice.

*(**ALICE** stops, looking at him.)*

ALICE. This is good, I'm happy for you.

(Pause.)

CONNOR. Look I –… Nothing's for sure yet, it was just a phone call, and I don't have to take the job even if they offer it to me.

ALICE. That's fine.

(Pause. She looks at him.)

CONNOR. Are you –?

ALICE. I'm fine, I –.

(Pause.)

I just would have appreciated your company there at the funeral today. Scotty was a methhead and a loser, but he was the last person in this entire family that wanted to have any relationship with me at all.

(Pause. She turns to go.)

CONNOR. I'm sorry –

ALICE. I'm hot, I'm just changing out of these black clothes, just –.

*(She leaves. **CONNOR** watches her go. Silence.)*

(Finally:)

CONNOR. Dammit.

(Silence.)

MARNIE. You're not –? Are you thinking of leaving because of me, or –?

CONNOR. No, no, I –.

(Pause.)

I mean it's not even for sure, it's...

(Pause.)

MARNIE. Are you gonna take it?

CONNOR. I just put my name in for it, they / haven't –

MARNIE. I know, but –. If you get it.

(Pause.)

CONNOR. I don't know. It's a little late for me to reinvent myself.

(Pause, checks watch.)

I got a shift at Walgreens in twenty minutes.

*(He exits. **MARNIE** watches him go.)*

Scene Five

(Nearing dawn. **MARNIE**, *having not slept at all, is standing, looking at the sunrise. Her cell phone is in one hand, an old cassette tape in the other.)*

(Finally, she looks at her phone, makes a call. She holds the phone to her ear, taking a few deep breaths. She waits.)

(The voicemail picks up; she considers hanging up, but doesn't.)

MARNIE. Hi, uh. Hi James. I'm leaving you a voicemail – obviously. I'm not surprised you didn't pick up, I wouldn't pick up either, I –... I'm sorry I've been ignoring you for two days. I really am, it was shitty of me, and I'm sorry.

(Looking at the tape in her hand.)

James, I haven't been totally – honest with you. I think I was scared to be honest with you, I didn't know what you would –... And I've been trying to get the courage up to actually talk to you, I think that's why I finally started listening to these tapes my mom made, to see if I could –... I don't know, I'm not like – looking for an answer, but just – something. And now I'm at the last tape, when she gets to the Pacific – and I can't bring myself to finish it.

(Pause.)

I think I'm realizing – I need to do this alone. I know I'm not making sense, I –...

(Pause.)

I can't move in with you.

(Short pause.)

I'm sorry. That's what I'm trying to say. I – can't move in with you.

(Short pause.)

MARNIE. I hope this recorded.

(Pause. She looks at her cell phone, hangs up, takes a deep breath. She looks at the tape in her hand.)

*(Slowly **ALICE** enters from the back, wearing a bathrobe. She looks at **MARNIE**.)*

*(Without looking at **ALICE**.)* Did you hear all of that?

(Pause. She puts the tape down.)

ALICE. I got the gist.

*(She comes downstage, approaching **MARNIE**. They both look out toward the river. A small firework goes off in the distance.)*

Lord, people are up late. What was that, a crackling ball? Sounded like one.

MARNIE. Cat tail.

*(Pause. **ALICE** gets next to **MARNIE**, bends down.)*

ALICE. Oof, my knee.

*(She sits on the ground beside **MARNIE**. Pause.)*

MARNIE. I think I might have –...

(Pause.)

I might have just alienated the last person I had left.

(Pause.)

ALICE. Was he good-looking?

MARNIE. *That's* your first question?

ALICE. Alright, what does he do, then?

MARNIE. He's getting his masters right now. Art history.

ALICE. Hm.

(Pause.)

MARNIE. He's really nice.

ALICE. So he's not very handsome then.

MARNIE. I didn't say that.

ALICE. You led with him being intelligent and nice, that means he's strange-looking.

MARNIE. He's not *strange-looking*, he just –. He just needs to use an exfoliant.

> *(Pause. Another firework goes off in the distance.)*

ALICE. You should have seen your grandfather when he was your age, you would have thrown yourself at him.

MARNIE. Ew.

> *(Pause.)*

Did he have a boat? I remember him taking me out on the river in a boat?

ALICE. He loved that thing, took it out every weekend, even when it was freezing outside. I swear, he *planned* to have that heart attack when he was out on the water. It's just like him, fit him so well.

> *(Pause.)*

MARNIE. People in our family sort of have a knack for dying dramatically, don't they?

> *(Pause.)*

ALICE. Yeah. I guess they do.

> *(Pause. Another firework goes off in the distance. They watch.)*

MARNIE. Do you know much about your great-grandpa? The guy who first homesteaded here?

> *(Pause.)*

ALICE. Great-great.

> *(Pause.)*

Not a lot. Family lore is when he learned his father was a cousin of Meriwether Lewis he was inspired to come out here, move out his whole family from Virginia.

MARNIE. Did he *know* Meriwether Lewis, or –?

ALICE. I think they had met at some point, but, I don't think they knew each other very well. Lewis was murdered shortly after he finished the expedition, when he was still young.

(Pause.)

MARNIE. Murdered?

ALICE. While he was traveling back to the East Coast, to settle some accounts.

(Pause.)

MARNIE. He killed himself.

(Pause.)

You know that Meriwether Lewis killed himself, right?

ALICE. No, see –. See that's not true –

MARNIE. He had all that debt from when he was governor of the upper Louisiana Territory, and he was like a heavy drinker –

ALICE. He was *murdered* for his *money* while traveling east, everyone knows that.

MARNIE. No, everyone does *not* know that, even William Clark and Thomas Jefferson accepted the fact that he committed / suicide –

ALICE. No one saw him shoot himself, / Marnie –

MARNIE. He was *alone* in his hotel room with a gun, and the innkeeper said he had been acting strangely the night before, talking to himself –

ALICE. It's these stupid *historians* insisting that he killed himself, they don't care about the facts, they just want a juicy –...

*(Pause, looking at **MARNIE**.)*

How the heck do you know all that, anyway?

(Pause.)

MARNIE. I mean I was a history major.

ALICE. Learn a lot about Meriwether Lewis in that half a semester, did ya?

(Pause. Another firework goes off in the distance. ALICE and MARNIE turn to it, watching.)

That's a nice one.

MARNIE. It's okay.

(Silence. They watch.)

When Mom left to walk the trail, did she –...?

(Pause.)

I remember being told that Mom had left to walk the trail, I remember that. Grandpa told me, I think. He said Mom was doing something she always wanted to do, and that she'd be back –

ALICE. Catherine was struggling with a lot of things that we didn't understand at the time –

MARNIE. Did she tell anyone that she was leaving? Or did she just, like – disappear?

(Pause. ALICE looks away.)

ALICE. Your mom loved you very much. That's what matters. That's what you should remember.

(Another firework goes off in the distance. They watch. Silence.)

MARNIE. When I was like six or seven, Mom gave me this book, this like – pop-up book about Lewis and Clark? You remember that?

ALICE. Sure, you loved that thing.

MARNIE. You pull the little tab and you could make them go down a river in a canoe or whatever, pull another tab to make them shoot buffalo and trap beaver. On another page you could make them wave at these Indians who are smiling back at them and welcoming them into their teepees. And knowing that I was related to this guy, it felt so –...

(Pause.)

MARNIE. And then you grow up and you find out that Lewis basically stole millions of acres, paved the way for genocide, ended up becoming a drunk who couldn't pay his bills and eventually shot himself.

(Pause.)

ALICE. Yeah, well. History is different when you're six years old. They don't tell you the truth until you're at least fifteen. And even then, they leave out the bad parts.

MARNIE. Yeah.

(Pause. Another small firework goes off.)

ALICE. Now that's a crackling ball.

MARNIE. Obviously.

(Pause. They continue to watch.)

Darkness

(As before, we hear the sounds of wind, birds, etc., accompanied by the sound of a rushing river.)

(A long silence as we listen to the river.)

FEMALE VOICE. I'm –...

(Pause.)

I'm looking at a deer, right now, this deer on the opposite side of the river. Or not like a deer, like a baby deer, a fawn. A little fawn, about the size of a dog.

(Pause.)

I've actually been standing here for a while now, it's –... Oh, I guess two hours. I've been standing here for two hours watching it, it's just sort of grazing, walking around, and –. I've been waiting for its mother to come back but I don't see it anywhere. It doesn't look like it's in trouble or anything, it's just – grazing, but it –...

(Pause. We hear the sound of rapid footsteps.)

Anyway, I'm not sure why I –... I'm on the Columbia now! Hiking alongside its coruscating waters. I think I'm near the Rock Fort Campsite. Which means I'm not far from Portland, so I'm –...

(Pause.)

I guess I'm getting closer. I guess I can sort of see the end.

Scene Six

(Late afternoon. **CONNOR** *holds a packed duffel,* **ALICE** *sits on her lawn chair.)*

CONNOR. I mean Lord knows if I'm even going to like it there, it's –. I mean I haven't been to southern Idaho in more than a decade, I don't even *remember* the last time I was in Pocatello, God knows if / it –

ALICE. Oh be quiet, you'll like it. You'll like the job, / you'll like the town.

CONNOR. Well I'm just not sure about that. And anyway I'll be back in a week or so to get my stuff –

ALICE. What stuff? You don't have any stuff.

CONNOR. I'll be back, Alice.

> *(Pause.)*

You sure you're okay with me taking the pickup? That old Chevy's falling apart, are you sure it even turns over?

ALICE. It'll be fine, I'll get it to the shop tomorrow, it'll get me to the Costco and back. I'm just worried about you driving a stick shift, you're / gonna kill someone.

CONNOR. I drove a stick shift for twelve years.

ALICE. You took out that mailbox with my pickup last year –

CONNOR. I didn't "take it out," God, I just –

ALICE. *And* you totaled that Mazda or / whatever it was.

CONNOR. Subaru and that wasn't my fault the stupid El Camino / ran the stop sign –

ALICE. Okay okay, just –.

> *(Pause.)*

Just be careful. I still don't think it's a good idea for you to take off today. It's the fourth, people are gonna be drinking and driving / like idiots –

CONNOR. It'll be fine, it'll be a nice drive –

ALICE. If you wait until morning then you'll get there at a reasonable / time –

CONNOR. If I don't leave right now, I'm not sure I'm gonna leave at all. I've got just enough nerve right at this second, I don't know where I'm gonna be tomorrow.

(They look at each other for a moment.)

(Silence.)

ALICE. Alright, enough. Go. Don't break my pickup.

(She takes car keys out of her pocket, throws them to **CONNOR**. *He catches them.)*

(He looks at her. Pause.)

What?

CONNOR. I'm just thinking, I –...

(Pause.)

Alice, when I moved here nine years ago or whatever, I was –. I was in a really bad place, and you didn't have to take me in like that, you really didn't –

ALICE. Oh God, what is this? What are you doing?

CONNOR. I just – you really helped me out, and it meant a lot to me –

ALICE. You helped me out too! The medical bills?

CONNOR. I know, but that was later. When you let me move in, I was the one who didn't have a dollar to my name, but you opened your doors to me, and it –... This is just *hard* for me –

ALICE. What, are you driving off a bridge? You're just moving to a different town! A different town in Idaho!

CONNOR. It's a ten-hour drive, Alice, it's not like we're / gonna see each other every weekend –

ALICE. *Ten hours* to Pocatello?! You driving a golf cart?!

CONNOR. *Dammit, Alice, would you just let me –!*

(Pause. They look at one another.)

ALICE. Alright, get it over with.

(Pause.)

CONNOR. I never felt at home here, in Lewiston.

(Pause.)

CONNOR. I was born here, I never lived anywhere else in my life, but – I never felt at home. I never felt comfortable, I never felt like I –... But – I felt at home *here*. With you. So, thank you.

(Pause.)

And – I'll miss you.

(Pause.)

That's it.

*(Pause. **ALICE** nods, smiles slightly.)*

ALICE. Okay then.

*(Pause. **CONNOR** looks back up to the house.)*

CONNOR. Tell Marnie I said bye?

ALICE. Well I imagine you might see her when you come back for your stuff.

(Pause.)

CONNOR. She's staying?

ALICE. Well I'm not saying *that*, I –. She just might be here for a few more days. Things have been a little – easier between the two of us, and maybe –.

*(Pause. **CONNOR** looks at her.)*

CONNOR. I see.

(He looks away.)

ALICE. What?

CONNOR. No, it's –. That's really great, and I should get on the road –

ALICE. For heaven's sake, Connor, are you *jealous*?

*(Pause. **CONNOR** looks at her.)*

CONNOR. *Jealous?*

ALICE. I'm not *replacing* you or anything.

CONNOR. That is *not* what I'm –...

(Pause. He thinks, puts his bag down. He looks at **ALICE**.*)*

Alice, for almost twenty years, my dad and I lived in houses that were less than thirty feet apart from one another, I saw him almost every day. If you would've asked me about our relationship before he died, I would have told you we had a great relationship, that we were very close. Wasn't until after he died that I found out what was really going on, that every day when I went to work he headed to the casino on the reservation, gambled away his savings. Took a loan out on the house, borrowed from three or four cousins, and –... But I didn't know it. I'd go over almost every night, make him dinner, bring him groceries, and I had no idea.

ALICE. What does this / have to do with –?

CONNOR. And now, if you were to ask me about my relationship with my dad? I would say that there was an *ocean* between us. And it was on me too, I never allowed him to really know me either, I only showed him the parts of myself that wouldn't *bother* him, the parts that were *acceptable*, that were –.

(Pause.)

ALICE. Connor, I don't know what you're getting at, but if you –

CONNOR. How much money have you given that girl?

(Silence.)

Ally I'm not an idiot. You sold close to two hundred acres, you'd be able to at least make your mortgage if you needed to. You basically funded that whole urban farm thing of hers, all the while letting her think the money was from her mom. And now she's here, and she's listening to Catherine's tapes – have *you* ever even listened to them?

(Pause.)

Look, I'm rooting for you guys. I think it's great she's back here. But – I just want you to think about what

Marnie might say in thirty years if someone asked her about her relationship with her grandma.

> (**ALICE** *looks at him. Silence.*)

I'll see you soon.

> (*He exits.* **ALICE** *watches him go.*)
>
> (*The sound of a door closing, the pickup driving away.*)
>
> (**ALICE** *looks out toward the river, lost in thought.*)

Scene Seven

(Later, near-darkness outside. **ALICE** *sits on her lawn chair, staring out toward the river.)*

(After a moment **MARNIE** *enters, just woken up. She carries the tape player from before.)*

MARNIE. Hey.

> *(Pause.)*

You okay?

> *(Pause. She puts the tape player down.)*

ALICE. Yeah, I'm –. I'm fine.

> *(Pause.)*

MARNIE. You get any customers?

ALICE. No, not –. A few, earlier. Not many.

MARNIE. I can't believe I just slept that long.

ALICE. You needed sleep.

MARNIE. Yeah, I guess.

> *(Pause.)*

Are you sure you're okay?

ALICE. Yes, I'm fine.

> *(Pause.)*

MARNIE. Oh. Connor left, didn't he?

> *(***ALICE** *looks at her.)*

ALICE. Yes, he –. He's left.

> *(Pause.* **MARNIE** *goes to her.)*

MARNIE. You know, I think it'll be good for him.

ALICE. Sure.

MARNIE. And you'll see him again.

ALICE. Yes, I –. Thank you.

> *(***MARNIE** *takes a few steps forward, looking toward the river.)*

MARNIE. I've been listening to some of the recordings from when she was passing right through here on her way to the coast? She used this word – "desultory." It was something about a beaver she saw just sitting near this river not doing anything, "I saw this desultory beaver."

(*Pause.*)

I'd forgotten she used words like that. I remember thinking that when I was a mom I wanted to use words like that, I –...

(*She trails off.* **ALICE** *looks at her.*)

ALICE. What?

(**MARNIE** *looks at* **ALICE.***)

MARNIE. I was thinking – if you haven't signed anything yet, maybe I could pay the mortgage for the next few months.

ALICE. You –?

MARNIE. Yeah. And – I was looking out back, there's a few acres where we could do some planting.

(*Pause.* **ALICE** *looks at* **MARNIE,** *struggling.*)

I mean just something simple, something to –. I mean if I was able to turn some old house in Seattle into a farm, I can do it here. Twenty acres is a lot more / than –

ALICE. Marnie, you –...

(*She turns away from* **MARNIE.***)

Look around, this isn't –. This place isn't what you remember –

MARNIE. I know, but –. Before you give it up, maybe we could at least try to do something with it, keep it in the family –

ALICE. It wouldn't –... It wouldn't work, Marnie –

MARNIE. Why not? I have money –

ALICE. No, you –. You aren't thinking clearly. How long will that last? If you want to stay here for a few days, that's fine, but eventually you're going to have to go home, you –

MARNIE. You don't understand, it's not that simple, I –...

> *(Pause.)*

I'm pregnant.

> *(**ALICE** looks at her. Pause.)*

ALICE. You're –?

MARNIE. And I think I – feel *good* about it. When I first got here, I wasn't even sure if I wanted to keep it, but now I actually –... I finally feel good about it.

> *(Pause. **ALICE** struggles.)*

I know it's crazy, but –. I mean Mom was my age when she had me, and I just –. I mean, this is what I always wanted, I wanted to be *here*, to like – carry on the family. Just like what you told Mom when she was little, what you told me when I was little. Maybe we can just like get past all the bullshit, start this again?

> *(Pause. **ALICE** looks at her.)*

ALICE. You have to leave.

> *(Pause.)*

MARNIE. What?

> *(**ALICE** looks away from her.)*

ALICE. Once the land sale is finished up I can send you money. It might take a few months, but I'll send you as much as I can.

MARNIE. I don't want your money –

ALICE. Just – use it for that kid. Go home to your boyfriend, he's that baby's father –

MARNIE. Believe me, he would *not* want to have a kid –

ALICE. *(Struggling.)* Well then just –, just –! This is my fault, I don't know why I've held on to these last twenty acres all this time, I should have sold all of this land the second I had the chance –

MARNIE. Why?

> *(Silence. **ALICE** looks at her.)*

ALICE. I swear to you, Marnie, I look at you and I see your mother and it *terrifies* me.

(*Pause.*)

When you and your father left for Tacoma, I thought – thank God, she'll find herself apart from this place. But now you –. And it's my fault, I know it is.

(*Pause.*)

Your father was convinced that I had pressured Catherine to stay here, to carry on the family. He thought that I was – caging her in... Maybe I was. Maybe it was a burden.

(*Pause.*)

The night Catherine got back from walking the trail, the night before it happened – she and I were down by the river. We were watching you dance around with sparklers, splash in the water. I made some comment about how the land would be yours someday, how all of it would be handed over to you.

(*Pause.*)

I looked at her and she was – *hollow*. I'd never seen her like that. I asked her what was wrong, she just said –. She said she had suddenly known something, when she finally got to the ocean. When she got to the Pacific.

(*Pause.*)

MARNIE. What did she –?

ALICE. I don't know. I just –... And now you want to bring another child into this, I –...

(*Pause.*)

Please, just *go*. Let this *end*.

(*Silence.*)

MARNIE. I've been trying to figure out why Mom sounds so different in these tapes, why it's so different from how I remember her. I realized, in these tapes, she actually sounds *happy*, she –.

(Short pause.)

I don't know why Mom –. But I can't just –, I have to find a way to move forward, I...

(Pause.)

Grandma, we have to believe that something good is *possible*, that it –... Right?

*(Silence. **ALICE** looks over the river.)*

ALICE. When I was a little girl, I used to hike up that ridge there, look over the land. I felt like it really – meant something.

(Silence.)

God, what a sad, tiny little life I've led.

*(Silence. **MARNIE** goes to the tapes, looking at them.)*

*(**MARNIE** takes out the tape she was holding at the beginning of Scene Five. She puts it in the player. **ALICE** watches her. **MARNIE** presses play.)*

*(In the background under the **FEMALE VOICE**, we hear the faint sounds of waves lapping against a rocky shore.)*

FEMALE VOICE. So I made it.

(Pause.)

I'm at the Pacific. The exact spot. Took me five weeks and – five days? Six?

(Long pause.)

Huh.

(Pause.)

I think I'm –... I think I'm realizing something, right now.

(Then, in the distance, over the river, large fireworks start to explode high up in the air, filling the stage with different-colored light.)

(**ALICE** *and* **MARNIE** *look up toward the sky, watching the fireworks.*)

FEMALE VOICE. I've been – imagining this moment for so long, ever since I was a girl, and now – here it is. This is the moment. I –... I thought I would feel a certain way, I'd feel different, something in me would change, that it would –...

(Pause.)

I guess I'm realizing that – I thought this would fix something. But it hasn't.

(Silence.)

I feel so – tiny. I'm realizing how tiny this trip has been. How tiny Meriwether Lewis must have felt when he got here.

(Pause.)

But I guess we don't think of him like that, do we? We think of him like he's some amazing pioneer, opening the West, helping to expand the country from ocean to ocean. Maybe that's the point. Maybe the real parts of him don't matter. Maybe –

(Short pause.)

I just saw a whale spout. I just saw –, right this second, out in the ocean.

(Pause.)

Maybe the trick is realizing that none of us really matter right now, none of us will ever get it right all the time. But hopefully the things we get right are the things that last. And maybe all the bad parts just die with us and the few little good parts of us survive.

(Pause.)

Marnie – I want you to know that there were a lot of moments on this trip, moments where I would wake up and watch the sunrise over the mountains, or see a baby moose crossing a river, and in those moments, I think I felt – happy. And that was nice. It felt new.

(MARNIE goes to ALICE. ALICE takes her hand. They watch the fireworks together.)

I think I'm turning back now. I'm turning this off and I'm – gonna head back to Lewiston now.

(Pause.)

That's it, I guess. I guess I'm done.

(Pause.)

I'm turning this off now.

(With a click, the tape player goes silent. One or two more fireworks explode before they stop completely and the stage goes dark.)

End of Play

PART TWO: CLARKSTON

CHARACTERS

JAKE – early to mid-twenties, male
CHRIS – early to mid-twenties, male
TRISHA – late thirties to early forties, female

SETTING

Various locations in and around a Costco in Clarkston, Washington. The store is on the edge of town, at the bank of the Snake River at the Idaho border.

The space should have the overall feeling of a parking lot. The different sections of the store should be created very simply, perhaps just with large metal shelves that rotate and move to denote the change in location. Every scene (except for the final scene) should have an oppressive, industrial feel.

Scene One

(Food Department: Snacks.)

(Massive metal shelves stocked intermittently with different brands of potato chips, all in gigantic bags, along with other items: licorice, candy corn, gummi bears, etc.)

*(**CHRIS** enters, pulling a palette on wheels with two large boxes full of items to be stocked. He is tall and broad, but not movie-star attractive by any means. He is followed by **JAKE**, nearly the physical opposite of **CHRIS**: small, thin, nearly delicate.)*

(They both wear Costco uniforms.)

CHRIS. Just tell Janet you don't want to work full shifts with him. If you get stuck with him for a few hours then you'll be fine, but if you get stuck with a / full shift –

JAKE. Wait he's not like dangerous though, is he?

CHRIS. Oh no, no. Well maybe.

JAKE. I mean was he in prison for something / really [bad] –?

CHRIS. It was just a drug thing, I think, I mean I'm sure he [isn't violent] –.

> *(Pause.)*

Sorry, I'm not trying to scare you.

> *(He starts taking the packing materials off one of the boxes, opening them up.)*

JAKE. No, I'm not, I'm –.

> *(Pause.)*

I'm just glad you're the one training me.

CHRIS. Yeah they don't let him train people anymore. Few years ago he was training this Nez Perce kid and he was being like *super* racist.

JAKE. Oh wow does he still work here?!

CHRIS. What?

JAKE. The –. The Indian –, Native American kid.

CHRIS. No. Why?

JAKE. Oh it's just –. That's cool. That he was a Native –, first peoples.

> (**CHRIS** *looks at him quizzically.* **JAKE** *smiles back awkwardly.*)

CHRIS. Where are you from again?

JAKE. Connecticut.

CHRIS. Okay.

JAKE. Town on the water called Waterford.

CHRIS. You don't have Indians there?

JAKE. I mean there's casinos.

> (*Awkward pause.* **CHRIS** *starts stocking the shelves.* **JAKE** *watches him for a moment, not doing anything.* **CHRIS** *stocks a few items, then looks at* **JAKE**.)

CHRIS. What?

JAKE. Oh, I'm just –. I mean I'm ready for the training.

> (*Pause.*)

CHRIS. Okay.

JAKE. So what do I do?

CHRIS. You take the stuff and put it on the shelf.

> (*Pause.*)

That's basically the training.

JAKE. Oh. Cool.

> (*He reaches into the box, takes out some items, and starts throwing them on the shelf haphazardly.*)

(**CHRIS** *stocks a few more items, looking at him.*)

CHRIS. I mean you have to like put them in rows.

JAKE. So there's more training.

(**CHRIS** *demonstrates shelving items.*)

CHRIS. Here, just –. Like this, you just want to be sure they're facing out. And don't stack them too deep, the customers can't get to them if you put them too far in. The larger boxes can go toward the back, then face the items toward the front.

JAKE. Oh awesome.

CHRIS. Yeah it's really not.

(*They both continue to stock items. Silence as they work. In the background, the somewhat loud whir of a forklift.*)

You're a long way from / home.

JAKE. What?

CHRIS. I said *you're a long way from home.*

JAKE. Oh. Yeah.

CHRIS. You out here for school?

JAKE. Oh no, I graduated a couple years ago.

CHRIS. You got family out here?

JAKE. *(Oddly excited.)* Well no but I have a family connection to the area!

(*Pause.*)

CHRIS. Okay?

(*The forklift sound suddenly cuts off.*)

JAKE. *(Still loud.)* I'm related to –!

(*Short pause.*)

(*Quieter.*) Actually I'm a descendant of William Clark.

(*Pause.*)

CHRIS. Oh.

JAKE. *(Smiling.)* Yeah.

CHRIS. Like the –?

JAKE. Yeah like Lewis and Clark. I'm related to him.

CHRIS. Huh, that's [interesting] –.

> *(Pause.)*

Sorry, what's your name again?

JAKE. Jake.

CHRIS. Jake.

> *(Pause.)*

Huh. Jake Clark, that's cool.

JAKE. Oh, no, it's –. Actually Clark isn't my last name.

CHRIS. Oh.

JAKE. I'm not like –… I mean I'm not like a *super direct* descendant. But my dad's cousin is a Clark.

CHRIS. So what's your last name?

JAKE. Baumgartner-Pepperdine.

> *(Pause.)*

My parents are assholes.

> *(They continue to stock.)*

You grow up in Clarkston?

CHRIS. Lewiston. Across the river.

JAKE. In Idaho!

CHRIS. Yep.

JAKE. That's really neat.

> *(Pause.)*

CHRIS. Okay.

> *(Silence. They continue to work.)*

So why'd you come out here?

> *(Pause.* **JAKE** *stops working for a moment, thinking.* **CHRIS** *looks at him.)*

You okay?

JAKE. Yeah, sorry, I –. I mean it's something I've always wanted to do. Go out west, follow the Lewis and Clark Trail. And I've never even seen the Pacific, it's ridiculous.

CHRIS. Huh. I've never seen it either.

(Pause.)

JAKE. Wait *really*?

CHRIS. Nope.

JAKE. You live like three hundred miles from the ocean and you've never seen it?

CHRIS. Just never had the chance, I guess.

JAKE. Wait so have you ever seen an ocean at all?

CHRIS. No. I mean like, photographs obviously, but –. No.

JAKE. Not even like a family trip?

CHRIS. My family doesn't –...

(Pause.)

I just haven't traveled a lot. Didn't even leave town for college.

JAKE. You went to –...?

CHRIS. LCSC, in Lewiston. English major. It was okay. I had like two good professors. Two and a half. Where'd you go?

JAKE. Bennington? It's like a little liberal arts school in Vermont.

CHRIS. What'd you major in?

JAKE. Post-Colonial Gender Studies.

(Pause.)

CHRIS. Huh.

(Pause.)

That's like – a thing you can study?

JAKE. The way the school works is you make up your own major.

CHRIS. Oh.

JAKE. It's actually pretty cool, the student is like really empowered there. At the end of each course the students grade the teacher.

CHRIS. And that – works?

JAKE. Yeah it's great. I mean who's to say that the professor knows more than their students?

CHRIS. Isn't it like – their *job* to know more than their students?

> *(Pause.* **JAKE** *doesn't know how to respond. They continue to work.)*

Emily's also one you don't want to get stuck with on the overnight. I mean she's fine and everything, she's totally nice, but she's just –... She has all these weird pictures of her iguana, it's like –. Anyway she's nice.

> *(Pause.)*

Here, why don't you open the other box?

> *(He hands* **JAKE** *his box cutter.)*

JAKE. Oh sure.

> *(He has a small, involuntary movement in his hand and drops the box cutter on the floor.* **CHRIS** *watches him.)*

CHRIS. You [okay]...?

JAKE. Yeah, sorry.

> *(He grabs the box cutter, then cuts the plastic tape off the box. He reaches over the box, struggling to open it. Finally, he gets the lid open.)*

> *(***CHRIS** *stops.)*

CHRIS. You know, you –.

> *(Pause.)*

You have to be able to lift sixty pounds?

> *(***JAKE** *looks at him. Pause.)*

I mean, the –. I'm not trying to be a dick but that's one of the requirements for the overnight stocker job, you have to be able to lift sixty pounds. If you can't then it just makes it really hard for whoever you're working with, they end up having to take up the / slack –

JAKE. I can lift sixty pounds. I can lift *more* than sixty / pounds.

CHRIS. Oh, cool, I was just [making sure] –

JAKE. I just accidentally dropped / the –

CHRIS. Okay, sorry.

> *(Pause.)*

Sorry.

> *(**JAKE** goes back to his work, quietly annoyed. He reaches into the box, pulling out large, heavy plastic tubs of popcorn kernels. Silence as they continue to stock.)*

> *(**CHRIS** feels bad, tries to re-engage **JAKE**.)*

We learned quite a bit about Lewis and Clark in elementary school. There was this guy who does like – impersonations of both Lewis and Clark? That's not the right word, he's not like an *actor*, he's a historian I think, but he –

> *(**JAKE** loses his grip on the tub; it falls to the floor, spilling everywhere. **CHRIS** sees him.)*

JAKE. *Fuck.*

CHRIS. Okay, why are you doing / that?

JAKE. I'm not –. I'm sorry, I just dropped it –

CHRIS. Again, I'm not trying to be a dick, but you can't do this job if you / can't even carry these –

JAKE. I'm fine, really –

CHRIS. There's other jobs here, the night shift sucks anyway –

JAKE. There's nothing else, I checked –

CHRIS. Look, lemme just grab Janet and we can / see if –

JAKE. I have Huntington's disease.

> (**CHRIS** *stops. Pause.*)

CHRIS. What?

JAKE. It's a degenerative neurological disease, and I have this variant of it called juvenile Huntington's, which means it sort of progresses quicker / than –

CHRIS. I mean I don't really know / what [this means] –

JAKE. So sometimes I might have to take a break or –, there's a thing called chorea where sometimes I have involuntary movements which is what that was, but *really* it's not that bad normally, I just need to be careful with –. Look it's not a big deal.

> (*Pause.*)

CHRIS. Did you tell Janet when she hired you?

JAKE. No.

CHRIS. So why did you tell me?

JAKE. Because if we're working together and you think I'm doing something weird or moving strangely, if I need to take a little break or something, / just –

CHRIS. But I mean you –. You think this is the best job for you?

JAKE. Look the pay is like twice what I'd be making at a McDonald's and probably even more than temping, if that even exists here, and they only had night stocker positions open, and I –.

> (*Pause.*)

And I just wanted to work – here.

> (*They stand awkwardly for a moment.*)

CHRIS. The health benefits are good.

> (*Pause.*)

I mean Costco, they have good benefits. The health plans are pretty good.

JAKE. Well there's no treatment for Huntington's so it doesn't really matter.

CHRIS. Really?

JAKE. I mean there's pills.

CHRIS. Do they help?

JAKE. Sort of. They don't really cure it, they just slow it down.

(Pause.)

CHRIS. Does it ever / go away?

JAKE. I'm gonna be dead before I'm thirty, pretty much for certain.

(Silence. He stares at his feet.)

(Re: the mess.) Is there like a broom or / dustpan –...?

CHRIS. Oh, yeah I can –. Here I can get it.

JAKE. If you just tell me where / it is –

CHRIS. No, I'll –. I'll get it.

> *(He exits. Silence apart from the sound of stocking and machinery in the background.)*
>
> *(**JAKE** is about to go back to shelving when his phone starts vibrating. He takes it out of his pocket, looks at it.)*
>
> *(It continues to buzz. He looks at it, not moving.)*
>
> *(**CHRIS** re-enters with a broom and dustpan.)*

Don't let Janet see you with that. She goes ballistic about the phones.

> *(**JAKE** quickly turns off the phone, puts it back in his pocket.)*

JAKE. I just – forgot to turn it off.

CHRIS. She caught me checking Facebook on the clock a few months ago and I swear she almost punched me in the face.

> *(He starts to clean up the mess.)*

Product loss isn't a big deal. Janet's actually pretty cool about the little stuff. Just don't do it with anything expensive.

JAKE. Sure.

CHRIS. This guy TJ ran a forklift over a box of digital cameras a few months ago. It was so fucking hilarious.

JAKE. Did he do it on purpose?

CHRIS. Said he didn't, but it happened like the day after Janet didn't give him a raise after his eval, so. He got fired pretty quick.

> (**JAKE** *tentatively goes back to stocking, not looking at* **CHRIS**. *Pause.*)

Hey.

> (**JAKE** *looks at him.*)

I won't tell anyone, okay?

> (*Pause.*)

Carrie does all the scheduling, I know her pretty well, so I'll make sure we do our shifts together. You need to take a break or whatever, you let me know. Just don't –. Try not to break a lot of stuff.

> (*He smiles at* **JAKE**, *continues to clean up the mess.* **JAKE** *stocks.*)

So you like –...? But why are you here?

JAKE. What do you mean?

CHRIS. If you just wanna see the ocean, why'd you stop in Clarkston, why work here?

> (*Pause.* **JAKE** *continues to stock, shelving large, plastic tubs of cheese puffs.*)

JAKE. I just felt like –. I wanted to stop for a while.

> (*Pause.*)

And I mean I thought maybe this would be good for me, I've never really had a job like this, like a – *real* job.

CHRIS. Huh.

JAKE. I mean if you think about it, all these stores like Costco in towns like this, hundreds of miles in between one another – maybe this is like the new West.

CHRIS. That's like the most depressing thing I've heard in a *while*.

JAKE. I don't think so. Maybe we're like the last American pioneers.

CHRIS. Cheese puffs go on the bottom.

JAKE. Oh.

> *(He moves the tubs to the correct row.)*
>
> (**CHRIS** *finishes mopping up the mess, starts to sweep up the popcorn kernels with the dustpan and brush.)*

Anyway I just needed to get away for a while I guess.

CHRIS. Sure.

JAKE. *And* I just got dumped.

CHRIS. That sucks.

JAKE. Yeah. I got the diagnosis, and a few months later he realizes we don't have a long-term future together so he just fucking –... Anyway. Asshole.

> (**CHRIS** *tenses up for a brief moment, keeps cleaning.* **JAKE** *senses his discomfort.)*

Oh, sorry.

CHRIS. No, it's [fine] –

JAKE. I don't even think about it anymore, I –. I've been out since I was like fifteen, both of my parents were like *hyper* okay with it, like to the point where it was a little annoying actually, but –. Anyway I don't really think about it very much. But I guess out here it's a bigger deal.

CHRIS. Nah, it's fine.

JAKE. I hope that wasn't weird of me to –

CHRIS. No, really, it's –.

> *(Pause.)*

It's really fine.

> *(A brief moment of recognition between them.* **CHRIS** *quickly ends it, finishes sweeping up the popcorn kernels. He motions offstage.)*

CHRIS. I'm just gonna –...

JAKE. Oh sure.

> (**CHRIS** *is about to exit, then turns back to* **JAKE**.)

CHRIS. It's actually not a bad place, you know?

> *(Pause.)*

Snake River is really beautiful, you can take boats down it when it's nice out. You'll get used to the smell of the paper mill after a few days.

> *(Pause.)*

I think you'll like it here.

Scene Two

*(**JAKE**, alone, sitting in the parking lot, his cell phone in his hand. He looks at it for a moment, then makes a call.)*

JAKE. Hi, Dad.

(Short pause.)

Okay please calm down, please –... I'm sorry, I know you've been calling, I'm –... Yes, I'm *fine*, I'm taking my meds, I'm safe.

(He stands up, paces aimlessly.)

No, I'm –. I'm not in Connecticut. I went – west.

(Short pause.)

Okay, look, I'm sorry for just leaving like that. And I understand that you're worried, and I know that this is selfish of me, I realize that, but please believe me when I say I *had* to do this, I had to do *something*, I had to –

(He has an involuntary movement in his leg, nearly trips and falls. He steadies himself for a second, takes a few breaths. He touches his leg, moves it a little bit, begins to calm down.)

No, I'm –. I'm still here.

(Pause.)

Okay, I'm not calling to tell you I'm coming home, I'm just calling to let you know that I'm safe.

(Pause.)

I mean I'm not sure I *am* coming back, I –...

(He sits back down. Pause.)

I don't know how to answer that, is *anyone* ever happy?

(Pause.)

Look, I have to –. I have to go. I'll call you.

(He hangs up, looking at his phone.)

Scene Three

(Much later, at the far edge of the parking lot, near the river.)

*(**JAKE** and **CHRIS** stand at a distance from one another. **JAKE** has been drinking. **CHRIS** looks around nervously.)*

(Awkward silence.)

CHRIS. Hey.

JAKE. Hey.

> *(Pause.)*

CHRIS. You okay?

JAKE. Fine.

CHRIS. You've been drinking?

JAKE. I'm not drunk.

CHRIS. It's okay, I don't care if you're / drunk.

JAKE. I'm not drunk.

CHRIS. Okay.

JAKE. Sometimes it's –. The chorea, it helps with it.

CHRIS. The what?

JAKE. It's like a symptom of the [disease] –. These involuntary movements, I was telling you before.

CHRIS. Oh, yeah.

> *(He looks around nervously.)*

JAKE. No one's gonna see us.

CHRIS. I'm not worried about that.

> *(Pause.)*

Look I'd invite you back to my place but it's –. You have a room or something?

JAKE. I'm staying in the hotel across the street.

CHRIS. Can we go there?

> *(**JAKE** looks out to the river.)*

JAKE. I kind of like the river. I like being by the river.

CHRIS. My truck is over there.

JAKE. No one can see us here. And no one's left in the store anyway.

CHRIS. Benji's around. The security guy?

JAKE. He's like a hundred. Plus he'd have to circle around the fence to see us –

CHRIS. I just don't want to get in / trouble with –

JAKE. Look we don't have to do this.

CHRIS. No, I –.

> *(Pause.)*

I wanna do this.

> *(**JAKE** takes a tentative step toward him. **CHRIS** is obviously nervous.)*
>
> *(Silence.)*

(Dirty.) So you want it?

> *(Pause.)*

JAKE. What?

CHRIS. *(Really bad at being dirty.)* I'm asking if you want it. Do you want what I have.

JAKE. …Sure.

CHRIS. It's ready for you.

> *(Awkward pause.)*

I'm talking about my / penis.

JAKE. Sure yep I know.

> *(Finally, **CHRIS** goes to him. He stands face to face with him. They look at one another.)*
>
> *(**JAKE** reaches for **CHRIS**' belt, **CHRIS** exhales, his shoulders falling.)*
>
> *(**JAKE** fiddles with the belt buckle.)*

I can't get the buckle.

> *(**CHRIS** looks.)*

CHRIS. No you have to like / open the –

JAKE. This is like the biggest buckle I've ever / seen –

CHRIS. Are you gonna make fun of me / or are you –?

JAKE. Sorry but I don't know how any self-respecting –

> *(A car horn in the distance.* **CHRIS** *jumps back, looking toward the noise, terrified.)*

Woah, calm down –

CHRIS. Sorry, sorry –

JAKE. It's just –. It's the other side of the store, no one can see us.

CHRIS. Sorry.

> *(Pause.)*

JAKE. Have you never done this before?

> *(Pause.)*

CHRIS. I mean I've been with guys.

JAKE. Yeah.

CHRIS. But just not –. Not like this.

> *(Pause, embarrassed.)*

Fuck.

> *(He looks away. Silence.)*

Look sorry this is weird, I'm being weird, we don't have to –

> *(***JAKE*** *goes to him, kissing him. It's awkward at first,* **CHRIS** *doesn't know what to do. Finally, he relaxes into it. It lasts for just a few moments. They look at one another.)*
>
> *(Pause.)*

You taste / like –

JAKE. It's root beer schnapps, I'm / sorry.

CHRIS. It's really disgusting.

JAKE. Yeah.

> *(Pause.)*

CHRIS. Do you do this – a lot?

JAKE. Are you asking me if I'm a slut?

CHRIS. No, I just –, I don't know / what to –

JAKE. We can do whatever you want. I mean not *whatever*, but –. You know.

> *(Pause. CHRIS goes to him. JAKE is about to reach for CHRIS' belt when CHRIS gets down on his knees. He begins to undo JAKE's belt. JAKE tenses up.)*
>
> *(CHRIS undoes JAKE's belt, is about to unbutton his pants when JAKE suddenly turns away from him, takes a few steps away, becoming upset.)*
>
> *(Pause.)*

Shit.

> *(He buttons his belt.)*

CHRIS. I'm sorry, I / didn't mean –

JAKE. No, it's –. It's me.

> *(Pause.)*

I thought I could do this.

CHRIS. It's cool –

JAKE. *No it's not it's –.*

> *(Pause.)*

I thought I could handle it and then I got nervous and I drank these disgusting root beer shots to calm myself down and now I just feel sick.

> *(Pause.)*

CHRIS. Wait are you –? Have you never done this before?

JAKE. Look, to be honest up until now I've been borderline puritanical, I wouldn't even have sex with my boyfriend until we'd been dating for –. I've just always been that way and I thought maybe *one fucking time* I could just –...

(He looks out toward the river. He sits down on the asphalt.)

JAKE. You have this idea in your head of the person you could be – but then it turns out you're just the same asshole you've always been.

*(Silence. **CHRIS** goes to him.)*

CHRIS. Look, it's –. It's no big deal, I mean I don't know if I could have done this either –

JAKE. You know back in 1805 William Clark was camping, *right here*. Right where this parking lot is now.

(Pause, looking.)

They'd been traveling for like a year and a half. And they camped here. The confluence of the Clearwater and Snake Rivers. They were like – the *first people* to see it.

*(Pause. **CHRIS** looks.)*

CHRIS. I mean except for like *all* the Indians.

JAKE. Right.

(Pause.)

I'm not racist.

CHRIS. No I know.

(Pause.)

Also didn't like a lot of French trappers and / Spanish –?

JAKE. *Point is*, they just –. I mean they were like *doing* something.

(Pause.)

I wonder if they knew then that someday there wouldn't be any more pioneers. That like two hundred years later pretty much no matter where you live in America, you have a car and can drive to Costco.

CHRIS. I mean that's what they wanted, right? Make it so America reached this far. Make it so people could live out here and be comfortable and happy.

JAKE. Are *you* comfortable and happy?

(Silence.)

CHRIS. Look, I'm gonna [go home] –. Let's forget this happened, I don't want it to be weird at work or / anything –

JAKE. How deep do you think it is?

CHRIS. What?

JAKE. The river, right here. How deep do you think it is?

> *(**CHRIS** looks out toward the river.)*

CHRIS. I don't know. I mean pretty deep. Toward the middle – thirty feet? More? I'm sort of guessing.

JAKE. Huh.

> *(He stands up, his eyes fixed on the water.)*

CHRIS. Are you / okay?

JAKE. If I walked into it would you wait an hour or so before you called the police?

> *(Pause.)*

CHRIS. Wait, what?

JAKE. Like just wait a while so you know that I'm...

CHRIS. Wait, you're gonna –...?

> *(Pause.)*

JAKE. *(Oddly unsure.)* I think so?

> *(He looks out to the river. **CHRIS** watches him. Silence.)*

CHRIS. This isn't –...

> *(Pause.)*

> *This is totally unfair.*

JAKE. I'm sorry.

CHRIS. I mean this is –... I mean this is, like –... You're asking for help, right?

> *(**JAKE** looks at him.)*

JAKE. No. I really don't want that. I really, really don't / want your help.

CHRIS. *Well then I don't know what* –. I just don't know what you expect me to do here –

JAKE. I know I've just met you and this is awkward and I'm sorry but I think the best thing you could do for me right now is watch me go into the water and make sure I don't come out. Make sure I don't fail at it like I do at everything else.

> *(Pause.)*

Like twenty minutes?

> *(He looks back out to the water. He takes a step toward the river.* **CHRIS** *takes a step toward him.)*

CHRIS. Wait, you –...

> *(**JAKE** stops, still looking at the river.)*
>
> *(**CHRIS** thinks, changes tactics.)*

Alright then, fine. Do it.

> *(**JAKE** looks at him.)*

Go for it. I'll make sure you don't come out. Go ahead.

> *(Pause.)*

JAKE. Okay.

> *(He starts walking toward the river.)*

CHRIS. *NO WAIT JESUS* –

> *(**JAKE** stops, looks at him.)*

I thought that would work for some reason.

> *(Short pause.)*

I'm a moron.

> *(**JAKE** smiles despite himself.* **CHRIS** *is heartened by it. Pause.)*

I mean is it –? Is it because of the disease, the –?

JAKE. No, it's –... I mean that's part of it, sure, but the Huntington's just like –... What's that phrase? It – put it "into stark relief," that's it. It put it into stark relief.

(Pause, looking at **CHRIS**.*)*

I mean have you ever been like *certain* that nothing you do is ever going to amount to anything? Have you ever looked at your life and been one hundred percent certain that when you die the world will be *no different*? I have never made, and will never make, any discernible contribution to society. I have a degree in *Post-Colonial Gender Studies*.

(Silence.)

CHRIS. You know I wanna be a writer.

JAKE. A writer?

CHRIS. Yeah, like –. Fiction writer. I write short stories. Maybe a novel someday, hopefully.

JAKE. Huh.

CHRIS. Yeah, you know the Iowa Writers' Workshop? Have you ever heard of it?

JAKE. Maybe.

CHRIS. It's a master's degree program, like the best in the country for fiction writing. I applied this year. And I think I have a good chance, actually, I wrote the head of the program an e-mail and she actually responded, she said that she was "looking forward" to reading my application.

JAKE. That's – good.

CHRIS. Anyway, I just think that –. I mean like if I write something, like I write something that gets published, and –. I mean I don't have to get famous or rich or anything, I just think if someday someone in a bookshop or a library or whatever pulls out my book and reads one of my stories and *likes* it then I –. I mean then I've done something.

(Pause.)

I'm just saying, I think there are like different ways to contribute. To society.

(Silence. **JAKE** *looks out toward the river.)*

JAKE. It's a terrible time to be alive. There's just nothing left to discover.

(Silence.)

I'm gonna just sit here for a while.

CHRIS. Yeah, me too.

*(He sits down next to **JAKE**.)*

JAKE. You really don't have / to –

CHRIS. Sun's gonna come up soon, it's nice.

*(Pause. **JAKE** looks out to the river, feels a gust of wind. He smiles a little.)*

JAKE. *(Quietly.)* "A cool morning wind from the east."

CHRIS. What?

JAKE. It's –. I was reading some of the journals earlier. William Clark's journals from when they got to the Snake River, around here. It starts like, "a cool morning wind from the east."

CHRIS. Huh.

*(Pause. **JAKE** thinks.)*

JAKE. "Had examined and dried all our clothes and other articles. Laid out a small assortment of articles as those Indians were fond of to trade with for provisions."

*(**CHRIS** watches him. **JAKE** closes his eyes.)*

"Captain Lewis getting much better. Several Indians visit us from different tribes."

(Pause.)

"Our hunters killed nothing today. Nothing to eat except a little dried fish."

(Pause.)

"Warm evening."

*(**CHRIS** continues to watch him. **JAKE** takes a deep breath.)*

Scene Four

(The next night, in the parking lot near the store. **TRISHA**, *wearing a Denny's uniform, nervously smokes a cigarette and holds a tote bag.)*

*(***CHRIS*** *looks at her, keeping his distance.)*

(A silence between them.)

CHRIS. We gonna do this every week?

TRISHA. You tell me, hon.

> *(She stubs out her cigarette, extends the tote bag toward* **CHRIS**.*)*

I got you some groceries.

CHRIS. I don't –.

> *(Pause.)*

Thank you, but I don't need groceries, I've told / you that.

TRISHA. It's just a few little things, the tuna you like and / the –

CHRIS. I don't want you buying things for me, you need to save your / money –

TRISHA. I'd really just like to feel like your mom? Just once in a while?

> *(Pause.)*

CHRIS. When I said I didn't want to see you for a while, I meant that I needed some / time –

TRISHA. Well I've been keeping my distance, haven't I? You said you needed space, I gave you space, I just don't know why –...

> *(Pause.)*

Come back home, Chris? Please?

> *(Pause.)*

CHRIS. Have you used at all?

TRISHA. Chris –

CHRIS. Tell me the truth, since I left have / you –?

TRISHA. Nothing, not once. That's six months. You know that.

>   *(Pause.)*

CHRIS. That's good.

TRISHA. Yeah, it's –. It's good, I'm just the same boring old mom I was when you were little.

>   *(Extending the tote bag.)*

Here, just –. Let me feel like your mother for one goddam minute.

>   *(**CHRIS** moves to her, takes the tote bag.)*

CHRIS. Thanks.

>   *(He looks inside the tote bag. He reaches in, pulls out a small, worn stuffed dog. He looks at it.)*

TRISHA. *(Smiling.)* You didn't take Clancy with you, just thought he could –. He was your favorite, right? I mean more / than –

CHRIS. Please stop bringing me stuff from home, I don't –

>   *(Pause.)*

Yeah, he was my favorite.

TRISHA. You staying with anyone, you –? I mean are you – *seeing* someone?

CHRIS. Mom.

TRISHA. I just don't know where you're staying, I don't know what kind of people you're going home to –

CHRIS. I'm not –. I'm not seeing anyone.

>   *(Pause.)*

TRISHA. You just –. You be careful, you hear me?

CHRIS. I know.

TRISHA. Around here, you don't know what –. I mean you just don't know how people are / gonna react –

CHRIS. I said I know, Mom.

TRISHA. I knew this kid in high school, he got it real bad once, was at the Mill Tavern downtown and these guys –, he ended up in the hospital for a couple / nights –

CHRIS. *I know Mom, you've* [told me this already] –.

(Pause.)

I gotta clock in.

(He turns to exit.)

TRISHA. Jesus, Chris, would you please just gimme a chance? I just wanna talk to you.

(Pause.)

Listen, I told those guys they can't come around the house anymore. I'm serious, it's done, I told them after you left – they aren't allowed to be in my life anymore. You were right, they were bad for me, I just couldn't [see it] –.

(Pause.)

Look I'm not saying I didn't have a bad year, I'm not saying that I've made all the right choices. But I'm *better*, you know? I'm just asking you to – *acknowledge* that I'm doing better. I'm here because I don't know where else I can talk to you, I'm damn near ready to follow you home at night just to make / sure you –

CHRIS. Do *not* follow me home –

TRISHA. *I'm not gonna follow you home –*

CHRIS. Look, do you just need money?

(Pause.)

TRISHA. Excuse me?

CHRIS. If you need some help this month, I can get you a couple hundred bucks, just please stop showing up / here and –

TRISHA. I *don't need money*, Chris, I –... Is that what you really think this is about?

CHRIS. Well?

(Pause. **TRISHA** *stares at him.)*

TRISHA. Rent's paid for the month, fridge is full. Trevor bumped me back up to forty hours a week at Denny's. We've been busy, the car show in town. Tips are good.

(Pause.)

CHRIS. That's – good.

TRISHA. Yeah. It is.

(Pause.)

CHRIS. I just didn't –... I wasn't sure if it was like two summers ago, I / didn't –

TRISHA. That happened *one time*, and I paid you back. I paid you back, right?

CHRIS. Yeah, you / paid me –

TRISHA. You think that's the worst I've ever seen?

(Pause.)

When you were nine or ten, when I lost my job at the paper mill? Your dad hadn't been in town for months, my parents said they'd only help me out with money if I sent you to live with them for good. Could you imagine that, you growing up with those people?

(Pause.)

I started working sixty hours a week, full-time at the Albertsons, part-time janitor at the hospital, all so we could keep a place where you had your own bedroom and you could still go to camp that summer. When you were at that camp I was mostly eating expired stuff the Albertsons was throwing away.

(Pause. **CHRIS** *looks at her.)*

CHRIS. I didn't know that.

(Pause.)

TRISHA. Listen, Chris – I know that it's been bad, it's not surprising you up and left like that. But I'm better now and it doesn't have to be like this is all I'm saying. We don't need to be living apart. We're a team, we always have been. We *need* each other, right?

(Pause.)

CHRIS. I don't know, I –.

(Pause.)

I just need some time.

TRISHA. Right, okay. I'll give you time.

(Pause.)

I can come by again tomorrow? Just to say hi?

(Pause.)

CHRIS. My shift tomorrow starts at ten.

(Pause.)

TRISHA. These night shifts aren't good for you.

CHRIS. Well it's money.

TRISHA. You remember a few years ago when I used to work nights? I don't think I slept for two years.

CHRIS. You didn't sleep for two years because you were always on meth, Mom.

(Silence.)

TRISHA. If you come by Denny's after work I can get you a free breakfast. Whatever you want. I know you don't like the food that much but it's free.

(Pause.)

CHRIS. I like the / pancakes.

TRISHA. Pancakes, I know it. You come by and I'll get you all the pancakes you want.

CHRIS. Let's just meet here tomorrow before my shift. Okay?

TRISHA. Okay.

(Pause. She moves toward him, her arms outstretched for a hug.)

(He looks at her for a moment, not moving.)

CHRIS. I'll see you later.

> *(He exits.* **TRISHA** *watches him go. She lowers her arms.)*

Scene Five

(Camping Gear: Tents and Tent Accessories.)

(A shelf littered with boxed-up tents of different sizes. One of the boxes has been opened. The box has the word "DISPLAY" written in large letters on the side of it. **CHRIS** *is unloading a palette, having just started.)*

*(***JAKE*** *enters, hurried and disheveled.)*

(He looks at **CHRIS**. **CHRIS** *gives him an awkward smile, avoiding eye contact.)*

JAKE. I'm really sorry –

CHRIS. It's okay.

JAKE. I didn't realize how late it / had gotten –

CHRIS. I'm not your boss, Jake, it's [fine] –. Janet's not too strict about it anyway, as long as you put in the hours.

JAKE. Okay. Cool. Sorry.

(Pause. **CHRIS** *looks away.)*

CHRIS. We, uh. We need to put one of the tents together for the display and shelve all / the –

JAKE. I can do the tent.

(Pause.)

CHRIS. You know how to [put together a tent] –?

JAKE. Yeah, sure.

*(***CHRIS*** *resumes shelving.* **JAKE** *goes into the box, takes out some of the parts, realizes he does not in fact know how to put together a tent.)*

*(***CHRIS*** *watches him.)*

CHRIS. You can start with the –

JAKE. I got it.

(Pause. He takes the tent cover, stands back, and unfurls it onto the floor, trying to make it seem like he knows what he's doing.)

JAKE. Look, um.

    (Short pause.)

I was drunk?

CHRIS. Well, yeah.

JAKE. It's just been a hard –. I got the diagnosis like six months ago, and my boyfriend broke up with me like four months after that, so it's just been – rough.

    (Pause.)

CHRIS. You know there are hotlines and prevention centers and people you can / talk to –

JAKE. No, I don't –. I mean I was just drunk.

CHRIS. So you weren't serious about it?

    (Pause.)

JAKE. Nah.

    *(**CHRIS** looks at him, knows he's lying. **JAKE** looks away, pulls the tent poles out of the box. He looks at them. He begins putting them together.)*

Was that your mom?

CHRIS. What?

JAKE. The lady in the parking lot.

    *(Pause. **CHRIS** looks away.)*

CHRIS. Yeah, she –. Yeah.

    (Pause.)

JAKE. My mom was on pain pills for like *most* of my childhood.

    *(Pause. **CHRIS** looks at him.)*

She fell down some concrete stairs when I was little, shattered her kneecap. After that she was always on pain pills, and for years it was like I didn't know what version of her I was gonna get when I came home from school.

CHRIS. / What?

JAKE. My parents got divorced when I was twelve and my mom finally went to rehab, now she likes to say that she was only on the pills because my dad was making her unhappy, which is complete bullshit, and now all she talks about is her fucking chakras and expelling toxins and –

CHRIS. Wait, you were listening to us?

(**JAKE** *looks at him, stops working.*)

JAKE. *No*, I just –. Look I just heard her say like *one thing* about / getting clean –

CHRIS. That's really not okay.

JAKE. I wasn't like *listening*, I was just –

CHRIS. I'm serious, don't eavesdrop on me and my fucking mom.

JAKE. Calm down – I mean you were having the conversation in a *public place*, it's not like I was –…

(*Pause.*)

Wow. Okay.

(*Pause. He is taken aback, goes back to the tent poles. He is awkwardly putting one of them together without threading it through first.*)

Are you not *out* or something?

CHRIS. How about we just work, how about that?

JAKE. Fine. Jesus.

(**CHRIS** *goes back to stocking, annoyed.* **JAKE** *rolls his eyes, goes back to the tent. The pole is now unreasonably long. He struggles to thread it through the tent.*)

CHRIS. Christ, just let me do it.

(**JAKE** *gives up, hands him the pole.* **CHRIS** *starts taking it apart, then threads it through the tent correctly.* **JAKE** *starts stocking the shelves.*)

CHRIS. I just don't want to be like *responsible* for you or anything.

>   *(Pause.)*

JAKE. What?

CHRIS. Like I just –. I don't think it's fair that I have to be the one that makes sure you don't [kill yourself] –.

>   *(Pause.)*

JAKE. *(Cold.)* You don't need to worry.

CHRIS. I'm not trying to be insensitive.

JAKE. Right.

CHRIS. I'm just saying I can't really –. I mean I barely know you –

JAKE. Yeah well I guess since I didn't suck your dick last night we're not –

>   *(**CHRIS** drops the tent, turning on **JAKE** angrily.)*

CHRIS. *Stop.*

>   *(**JAKE** backs away from him.)*

JAKE. *Jesus Christ...*

>   *(Pause. **CHRIS** regains himself.)*

CHRIS. Just shut up, okay?

>   *(Pause.)*

JAKE. Are you really *that far* in the closet?

CHRIS. Jake.

JAKE. What, you think we're gonna get arrested or / something?

CHRIS. What I think is you're not in fucking Connecticut.

>   *(Pause.)*

I am "out" to the people I *want* to be out to. So just [shut up] –.

>   *(He goes back to setting up the tent. **JAKE** looks at him for a moment, then goes back to work as well.)*

(Pause.)

You know Lewis and Clark were sort of douchebags, right?

*(**JAKE** looks at him. **CHRIS** continues to pitch the tent.)*

JAKE. What?

CHRIS. I'm just saying, they –. I mean I was reading some stuff online earlier today, it's not like they were –. I mean there had been plenty of people who had already been out here, it's not like they were like the *first* people / who saw –

JAKE. I never said they / were the first –

CHRIS. And they would approach all these Indian tribes and give them some stupid speech about how they –, like, how Thomas Jefferson was their new *chief* or something? And Clark had a fucking *slave* with him? Did you know that?

JAKE. *Yes*, I knew that, / I –

CHRIS. I don't know why we have to think they were so fucking *noble* or whatever, they were just sort of glorified colonialists claiming land for America that was "sold" to us by France even though they –

JAKE. Chris, what are you doing?

*(**CHRIS** looks at him, then goes back to working on the tent. He struggles to pitch it by himself. Silence.)*

*(**JAKE** slowly goes to **CHRIS**, helping him with the tent. **CHRIS** looks at him for a brief moment, then looks away. They pitch the tent together.)*

(Finally:)

CHRIS. You know I really do care about her.

(Pause.)

JAKE. Maybe you should tell her that.

(Pause.)

JAKE. And I know they were kind of assholes. Lewis and Clark. And I know Clark had a slave, and that's –.

(Pause.)

I just like the idea of them more than what they actually were I guess.

(They secure the second pole. The tent is pitched.)

CHRIS. There.

(Pause.)

JAKE. Looks okay.

CHRIS. Sort of.

*(Pause. He takes out the tent cover, handing it to **JAKE**. **JAKE** starts to put the cover on the tent.)*

*(**CHRIS** looks at the box. Pause.)*

It wasn't even made here. Manufactured in Shenzhen.

JAKE. That's a city?

CHRIS. Yeah, in China. I've read about it. This city that's nothing but industry, built really quickly. Thirty years ago it was a fishing village and now it's like this monster.

JAKE. Huh.

(He has some involuntary movement in his hand; he struggles to attach the tent cover.)

Goddammit...

*(**CHRIS** sees, going to him. He steadies **JAKE**'s hand, allowing him to secure the tent cover. They look at one another briefly.)*

*(**CHRIS** lets go of **JAKE**'s hand. Pause.)*

*(**CHRIS** takes a price tag off the shelf, affixes it to the tent. They both stand back, looking at it.)*

(Pause.)

It's a shitty tent.

CHRIS. Yeah it doesn't look very good.

Scene Six

*(Days later, after their shift, very early morning. **JAKE** and **CHRIS** are sitting in the parking lot with their backpacks. **CHRIS** is reading from a notebook.)*

CHRIS. "The fog washed over his boat in gigantic waves of blank space, deleting everything around him farther than fifteen feet. And as he reached for an oar to paddle himself back to the dock, he suddenly realized that the steady bleating of the foghorn had ceased. He hadn't –"

JAKE. Wait, is this –? It's scary?

CHRIS. Well, yeah, it's / kind of –

JAKE. Is this like a ghost story?

CHRIS. I mean there aren't any *ghosts* in it –

JAKE. But it's like scary, right?

CHRIS. I mean, sure, it's scary, but that's not like the point / of the –

JAKE. I just don't do well with scary stuff.

CHRIS. I can stop.

JAKE. Yeah maybe you should. No keep going. Sorry. Shut up.

*(Pause. **CHRIS** goes back to reading.)*

CHRIS. "...He suddenly realized that the steady bleating of the / foghorn –"

JAKE. Wait and you realize this is like *where I grew up*. A coast, with the cold, and the fog? You're writing about where I grew up.

CHRIS. Oh, yeah, I mean it could be a lot of places, / but –

JAKE. I thought you've never seen the ocean?

CHRIS. I haven't. I just like writing about it.

JAKE. Huh.

(Pause.)

I keep interrupting sorry keep going.

(CHRIS goes back to reading.)

CHRIS. "...He suddenly realized that the steady bleating of the foghorn had ceased. He hadn't noticed the precise moment it had stopped, but he suddenly felt its absence like he was missing a life preserver. The idea that he had suddenly floated out to sea far enough that he wasn't able to hear the foghorn was ridiculous, so he managed to convince himself that something had gone wrong with it, not him. But it wasn't until he grabbed a paddle that he realized – without the foghorn, he wasn't entirely sure what direction land was –"

(JAKE groans a bit.)

You realize I just made this up.

JAKE. No I mean it's good, I like it. When I grew up I was *petrified* of the ocean, so.

CHRIS. You grew up on the water and you were scared of it?

JAKE. When I was a kid I almost drowned.

CHRIS. Oh, wow.

JAKE. Yeah. And the thing about drowning is that it doesn't look anything like it does on TV, you don't yell and thrash around, you just –. My dad was like ten feet away from me, didn't even realize. Lifeguard finally saw what was going on, saved me.

(Pause.)

CHRIS. You want me to keep going?

JAKE. Oh yeah of course, I'm just –. I'm just ridiculous, I'm a mess. Keep going.

(Pause.)

(CHRIS resumes reading.)

CHRIS. "But being reasonably sure the dock was behind him a hundred or so feet, he reached for a paddle and put it into the water. In what felt like less than a second, the paddle was gone.

(JAKE groans again.)

CHRIS. "The moment had gone by so quickly that he had barely had time to process it. But he could have sworn there was some subtle force other than gravity that had pulled the oar down into the opaque waters."

JAKE. Oh god.

> *(He tenses up, hugging his knees.* **CHRIS** *enjoys his discomfort, taking it as a compliment.)*

CHRIS. "Pushing the thought out of his head as quickly as possible, he leaned over the side of the boat, putting his hand into the water, hoping that the oar was floating gently beneath the surface. The fog grew thicker and wetter and he stared down at the water, moving his hand back and forth. Then, leaning further over the edge of the boat –

JAKE. / *Eeeee –*

CHRIS. "– He stuck his hand farther into the water when, like a pair of flashlights being switched on, two bright yellow human eyes appeared in the water staring up / at him –"

JAKE. *(Standing up.)* Okay nope nope nope sorry nope.

CHRIS. *(Smiling.)* Sorry –

JAKE. Seriously stop reading.

CHRIS. I'm stopping, I stopped –

JAKE. Don't laugh at me it's not funny.

CHRIS. I'm not!

JAKE. That's like –.

> *(Pause.)*

Okay you managed to put like *all of my fears ever* into one story.

CHRIS. That's neat.

JAKE. No it isn't! I have to go back to my dark empty hotel room after this.

> **(CHRIS** *picks up a pipe that's sitting next to him, offers it to* **JAKE.)**

CHRIS. You want the last hit?

JAKE. *No,* I am –. I am *good.* I haven't smoked weed in months, I'm sort of freaking out.

CHRIS. I don't have to read the rest –

JAKE. No, I want –. I'm sorry, I know I'm being annoying, I want to hear the rest, but could you –. Just skip the scary stuff?

(Pause.)

CHRIS. Seriously?

JAKE. It's fucking *dark* and I don't want to think about two flashlight eyes / or whatever –!

CHRIS. But it's like –. I mean it's a scary story, I don't know / how to –

JAKE. Okay whatever just read it. Shut up. Read it read it read it.

(He sits back down, hugging his knees. **CHRIS** *looks at his notebook.)*

CHRIS. Okay.

"The eyes remained under the surface, unblinking, looking straight at him, and as he continued to stare back he realized the eyes had a deep sense of grief in them, a grief he recognized as his own. Suddenly the eyes weren't shocking and unexplainable, they were entirely recognizable, almost mundane, as familiar as his own eyes looking back at him in the mirror every morning. Suddenly these eyes, though jaundiced yellow and incandescent, were his own."

*(**JAKE** listens, unmoving.* **CHRIS** *looks at him.)*

You okay?

JAKE. Yeah, I'm –.

(Pause.)

Keep going.

(He sits near **CHRIS**, *listening intently as he watches the river in front of him.)*

CHRIS. "The grief that he recognized in those eyes was the grief he felt every night going home to his empty apartment, the grief he felt when he would drive his aging pickup to work, the grief he felt almost every moment of every day, the grief that somehow only seemed to go away when he was in his boat, on the water, in the fog. The haze continued to roll in, gaining a thickness that seemed impossible, and soon the ocean itself was shielded in white, and he could barely make out the end of his boat. As the whiteness closed in around him, covering his feet, then his legs, then his torso, the only thing that remained visible in the void were the two constant eyes staring up at him. Slowly, he no longer felt his boat beneath him, he no longer felt the clothes on his body. His five senses had been stripped from him one by one, the glowing yellow eyes his last connection to the world around him. And just as he had his last thought – the briefest thought of a smile – the eyes were extinguished."

> *(Silence. He puts the notebook away.* **JAKE** *looks at him.)*

That's it.

> *(Pause.)*

I mean it's just like a tiny short story. It's like my shortest. I think the last paragraph is sort of dumb, I / should –

JAKE. That was crazy.

> *(Pause.)*

I mean it was good, it was –. It was good.

CHRIS. Thanks.

JAKE. It was crazy though. The end is crazy.

> *(Pause.)*

What's it about?

> *(**CHRIS** thinks.)*

CHRIS. I mean I don't know. I don't know if it's about anything.

JAKE. Huh.

CHRIS. I guess when I write I don't try to have like one single point that I'm trying to make. I'm not trying to give a moral or something.

(Silence.)

JAKE. Wait – is it about suicide?

CHRIS. It's brand new, I don't know. Maybe it's too weird.

(Pause.)

JAKE. I think it's really good, I think you're gonna get in.

CHRIS. Really?

JAKE. Yeah totally.

CHRIS. It's really hard to get into. We'll see.

(Pause.)

So what do you wanna do?

JAKE. Like, now?

CHRIS. I mean like –. I mean what do you want to do in the future, after you go see the ocean?

(Pause.)

JAKE. I don't know. I mean I've only got like eight years, maybe, that's what they said. But toward the end it's not like it's gonna be easy for me to get around or –

CHRIS. Sorry, we don't have to talk / about it –

JAKE. Nah, it's –. It's fine. I mean it's a degenerative disease, so it'll take a while, but. Eventually it's –. It's not gonna be pretty. I'll lose control of my limbs, won't be able to walk, difficulty swallowing, talking, and –. I'll start to lose memories, they'll fragment and distort and then eventually full-blown dementia, and –.

(Pause.)

Basically my body is gonna forget how to be alive.

(Silence. Finally, he jumps up.)

Okay, another one!

CHRIS. What?

JAKE. Read me another story. I'm ready to be freaked out again.

CHRIS. Oh, naw –

JAKE. C'mon.

CHRIS. Why don't *you* read me something?

JAKE. Me?

CHRIS. Yeah, read me something from the journals, William Clark's journals. You've been reading them, right?

JAKE. I mean, I'm always reading them.

> *(Pause.)*

I don't think you'd like find them interesting.

CHRIS. C'mon, I wanna hear. Let's hear what your great-great whatever grandpa had to say.

JAKE. Cousin.

CHRIS. Whatever.

> *(Pause. **JAKE** opens up his bag, takes out a worn paperback book.)*

JAKE. You wanna hear about anything in particular?

CHRIS. You said he wrote some while he was around here, right? Read me that part.

JAKE. Okay then. Early October, 1805.

> *(He thumbs through the book a bit, lands on a page.)*

"Had all our horses, thirty-eight in number, collected and branded. Cut off their foretop and / delivered –"

CHRIS. What's "foretop"?

> *(**JAKE** shrugs.)*

JAKE. "– And delivered them to the two brothers and one son of one of the Chiefs who intents to" blah blah blah, stuff about horses…

> *(Skims.)*

"Captain Lewis and myself ate a supper of roots boiled, which filled us so full of wind that we were scarcely able to breathe all night."

CHRIS. It really says that?

JAKE. Yeah, diet was a big deal to them. It was like half the battle of being out here.

CHRIS. Huh.

JAKE. "I am very sick tonight, pain in stomach and the bowels owing to my diet. It is certainly the effects of my diet last night."

CHRIS. *(Laughs.)* Okay.

JAKE. "Tonight Captain Lewis and myself ate a supper of roots boiled, which swelled us in such a manner that we were scarcely able to breathe for several hours –"

CHRIS. Well stop eating the fuckin' boiled roots.

(They both start giggling, both fairly high by this point and getting silly.)

JAKE. "Several squars came with fish and roots which we purchased of them for beads –"

CHRIS. WHY ARE YOU BUYING MORE ROOTS?!

(Their giggling increases, becoming a laughing fit.)

JAKE. Okay, okay –

(They calm down, breathing.)

CHRIS. This is what you just sit and read all day?

JAKE. Yeah, I guess.

CHRIS. And you like it?

JAKE. Sure, it's –. I love it.

CHRIS. What's your favorite part?

*(**JAKE** continues to calm down, thinks.)*

JAKE. I mean everybody likes, "Ocean in View! O! The Joy!" It's what he said when he finally saw the Pacific. It's like printed on a quarter I think. It's famous.

CHRIS. That's your favorite?

JAKE. I guess.

(Pause.)

I mean I don't know. I like a lot of it.

CHRIS. I haven't thought about it very much, growing up here, but –. I mean thinking that we're sitting here right now, like right where they were two hundred years ago...

> *(Pause.* **JAKE** *thinks for a second. He looks toward the river, thinking.)*

What?

> *(***JAKE*** *looks around for another moment.)*

JAKE. Huh.

CHRIS. What?

JAKE. I just realized, they –... They weren't here. We're on the Washington side, they were on the Idaho side. I didn't even –... I didn't even realize it until just now.

> *(Pause.)*

They weren't here.

CHRIS. Huh.

> *(Pause.)*

I mean you can go to the other side, it's really easy, the bridge is just like a three-minute drive down there.

> *(***JAKE*** *continues to look at the river.)*
>
> *(A very long silence.)*
>
> *(Finally:)*

Are you / okay?

JAKE. "I took two men and set out in a small canoe and ascended the Columbia River ten miles to an Island near the starboard.

> *(Closing his eyes.)*

"The number of dead salmon on the shores and floating in the river is incredible to see. Passed three large lodges on the starboard side near which great number of salmon was drying on scaffolds. One of those mat lodges I entered, found it crowded with men, women, and children. I was furnished with a mat to sit on, and one man set about preparing me something to eat.

(Pause.)

"The people appear to live in a state of comparative happiness."

(Pause. He opens his eyes, looks out to the river.)

(Distant.) That's my favorite I guess.

*(**CHRIS** watches him.)*

Scene Seven

(The parking lot. **TRISHA** *waits for Chris, holding two gas station coffees, smoking a cigarette.)*

*(***JAKE*** *enters. He looks at* **TRISHA**. **TRISHA** *nods at him, smiles slightly, then looks away.)*

*(***JAKE*** *is about to walk past her, then makes a decision and goes to her.)*

JAKE. Hey.

(Pause. **TRISHA** *turns to him.)*

TRISHA. *(Confused.)* Hi?

JAKE. I'm, uh. I work with Chris?

TRISHA. Yeah?

JAKE. I'm a – friend of Chris?

(Pause.)

TRISHA. Oh.

JAKE. I mean I haven't been working here for very long but we've been –, we hang out and –. Anyway, hi.

(Pause.)

We just got off our shift, he should be out in a minute or so, he's just finishing up with some display stuff.

(Pause.)

TRISHA. How did you know that I was / his –?

JAKE. I saw you two talking in the parking lot the other night.

(Pause.)

I don't know him very well yet but I know that he's not like, *forthcoming* or whatever about what he's feeling but I know he cares about you and I – wanted you to know that. That's all.

(Pause. **TRISHA** *stubs out her cigarette, puts it back in the pack.)*

TRISHA. So he's told you all about me then.

JAKE. I mean, sort of –

TRISHA. Crazy drug addict, all that / stuff?

JAKE. *No*, he... He really hasn't, I'm just –. I'm just trying to say that he doesn't want to give up on you.

(*Pause.*)

TRISHA. He told you that?

JAKE. Yeah. He has.

(**TRISHA** *wanders aimlessly.*)

TRISHA. Yeah, well, he's got good reason to give up on me, I guess.

(*Pause.*)

I never gave up on him, though. And I could have, believe me. I had him when I was sixteen years old, I could've just sent him to live with his grandparents but I didn't, I refused to give up on him. I have given my *life* to that kid. When his dad left for good, I told him if he ever came back I'd take him down with our shotgun. He knew I meant it, too. One thing you *do not do* is threaten my child. You can do whatever you want to me, I can take whatever, but *not* my kid.

(*Short pause.*)

And look I may not be perfect, but neither is he.

JAKE. I mean I don't / really –

TRISHA. I don't know what he's told you about me, but that kid needs me just as much as I need him. Couple years ago he blew outta town, tried to move away, ended up calling me from a Super 8 down in Pocatello, totally freaked out. Drove *ten hours* to go and get him. So don't go thinking that he's some poor *victim* or / whatever –

JAKE. I don't think –. Look, sorry, I shouldn't have said anything, I'll just –...

(*He starts to exit, heading toward the Costco.*
TRISHA *takes a step toward him.*)

TRISHA. *Wait, I'm –.*

    *(**JAKE** stops.)*

I'm sorry, I shouldn't –.

    (Pause.)

He's my favorite guy in the world, but he's not as tough as he looks, you know? So do me a favor, just – make sure he's okay? Keep an eye out for him?

    (Pause.)

JAKE. Yeah, I'll –. I will.

    *(Silence. **TRISHA** takes a breath, regards **JAKE**.)*

TRISHA. So you two are –...?

    (Pause.)

Shit I'm just not used to this yet.

    (Pause.)

JAKE. *(Realizing.)* Oh, I –. I mean we're / not –

TRISHA. He staying with you?

JAKE. *No*, really we're not –

TRISHA. He find a decent place to stay?

JAKE. I mean, I think it's – fine. I think he's fine.

TRISHA. The place is okay, landlord okay?

JAKE. I mean I think it's fine, I don't think he's looking for something very permanent. If grad school works out, I mean.

TRISHA. What?

JAKE. I mean if he ends up going to Iowa, he's not –...

    *(**TRISHA** looks at him. **JAKE** realizes, stops himself.)*

TRISHA. He's applying to school? In Iowa?

    *(**JAKE** looks away.)*

JAKE. I don't –. *Shit.*

    (Awkward silence. He looks to the Costco.)

Look, I –. Chris'll be here soon, I'm gonna / head home –

TRISHA. I gotta say I'm sorta surprised though.

> *(She indicates* **JAKE**.*)*

JAKE. What?

TRISHA. I just didn't think he'd end up with someone so scrawny.

> *(Pause.)*

No offense.

> *(Pause.)*

JAKE. "Scrawny"?

TRISHA. No offense.

JAKE. When you say something that's completely offensive, saying "no offense" afterward doesn't make it any less completely / offensive.

TRISHA. Look whatever, he can be into whatever he / wants –

JAKE. Maybe *he's* the lucky one, did you ever think of that?

TRISHA. I'm sure / he is.

JAKE. My IQ is like almost 140.

TRISHA. Is it that high?

JAKE. *Yeah it's that high.* I took a test online.

TRISHA. Alright then.

JAKE. And I'm a descendant of *William Clark.*

TRISHA. No shit?

JAKE. *Yeah. So.*

> *(Pause.)*

I'm also *funny* and *charming* and *urbane* and –

> *(***CHRIS** *enters.)*

CHRIS. What the fuck?

JAKE. I was / just –

CHRIS. *(To* **JAKE**.*)* What are you doing?

JAKE. I'm sorry, I'll / just [go] –

TRISHA. I met your [boyfriend] –. I didn't think you were, whatever, *seeing* anyone.

CHRIS. *What?*

JAKE. / Oh my God –

TRISHA. I mean it's fine, he's cute. You can put 'im in your pocket.

JAKE. *(To* **TRISHA**.*)* Okay you need to stop because I am *not* that small –

CHRIS. JAKE.

> *(***JAKE*** stops, looks at him.)*

JAKE. Look I didn't say anything, she just / assumed –

CHRIS. *I'll see you tomorrow, Jake.*

> *(He doesn't look at* **JAKE**. **JAKE** *exits. Silence.)*

TRISHA. I'm sorry.

CHRIS. Mom.

> *(Pause.)*

TRISHA. He seems – nice.

> *(Pause. She smiles at him.* **CHRIS** *smiles despite himself.)*

CHRIS. Mom.

TRISHA. I like him! He's a little spitfire, I like him.

CHRIS. Oh my God, Mom, can we please / not –?

TRISHA. I just wanna know who you're –, you know! I'm your mom, I wanna make sure you're not seeing some weirdo, or –

CHRIS. Well maybe it's none of your business, and I know it makes you uncomfortable anyway, so maybe just –

TRISHA. Look, I think I'm being pretty good right now, I think I'm being pretty accepting. I know being gay in this town is hard, but it's not easy for me either. People think I did something wrong, like I was a bad mom, or –. This bitch Tanya I work with at Denny's? She actually said she was *praying* for you, you believe that? I told her what she could do with her damn –...

> *(Pause.)*

Anyway it's not easy for me either. And I'm trying, is all.

(Silence. **CHRIS** *softens.)*

CHRIS. You work yesterday?

TRISHA. Noon to eight.

CHRIS. Everything's – okay?

TRISHA. I mean Trevor's still a dick, I still say he's skimming from the tip pool, but –.

(Pause.)

Yeah, it's fine. Been sleeping like a rock.

CHRIS. That's good.

(Pause.)

Have you had – cravings or whatever?

TRISHA. Not one. I don't miss it at all.

(Pause.)

CHRIS. Have you looked into any of the NA programs that I showed you?

TRISHA. Chris, you know that isn't / for me –

CHRIS. If you're gonna do this then you need some support –

TRISHA. Well that's why I'm here, Chris.

CHRIS. Mom this can't all be about *me* –

TRISHA. I know that, I'm just saying –

*(***CHRIS** *turns to leave.)*

CHRIS. Okay, I can't have this conversation again, I'm going / home –

TRISHA. When were you gonna tell me about Iowa?

(Pause. **CHRIS** *turns to her.)*

CHRIS. He told you.

(Pause.)

TRISHA. Were you just gonna blow outta town without even saying goodbye, that was your plan?

CHRIS. Mom, it wasn't –. I just *applied*, I –… *Goddammit.*

(Pause.)

TRISHA. You know what, Chris? You don't need grad school. If you wanna get outta here, let's just *go*, leave town. You and me.

(*Pause.* **CHRIS** *looks at her.*)

CHRIS. You wanna just – leave?

TRISHA. Why not? Nothing keeping us here.

CHRIS. I have a job here –

TRISHA. You can get a job anywhere, so could I. Plenty of Costcos and Denny's out there. And nothing good ever came out of this town, especially for us. I've got some money saved up from the past couple months. Not a lot, but enough to get us settled.

CHRIS. Where would we go?

TRISHA. I don't know, does it even matter? I say we pack everything up, pick a direction, and just *go*. We're survivors, Chris, you know that – but we need to stick together.

I know you wanna get outta here, but you can't do that alone, you know that.

(*Pause.*)

Listen, if we find someplace to go, I'll –. I'll get into one of those NA programs you keep telling me about.

CHRIS. Really?

TRISHA. Yeah, why not? Couldn't hurt.

CHRIS. Seriously, if I go with you, you'll get help for this, / you'll –?

TRISHA. Hand to God, Chris.

(*Pause.*)

You don't have to decide right now, I know you've got your – friend here. But just think about it?

(*Pause.*)

CHRIS. I'll think about it.

TRISHA. Okay.

(She smiles at him. She outstretches her arms for a hug, as before.)

*(**CHRIS** looks at her for a moment, then goes to her, hugging her.)*

I love you.

CHRIS. I love you too, Mom.

TRISHA. I miss you so much.

CHRIS. I miss you too.

(Pause.)

I do.

(Pause. They hold one another.)

Scene Eight

(Electronics: Flat-Screen HD Televisions.)

(The next day. **JAKE** *is unpacking a box filled with various television accessories: universal remote controls, cords, etc.* **CHRIS** *enters with a palette, on top of which are several 80-inch flat-screen HD televisions, each in massive boxes.)*

*(***JAKE*** looks at him.* **CHRIS** *doesn't look back. Pause.)*

JAKE. Look, I'm sorry, I texted you over and over but / you –

CHRIS. *(Not looking at him.)* It's fine.

(Pause.)

JAKE. Are you really gonna ignore me the entire shift?

CHRIS. *(Re: the televisions.)* Can you lift these?

(Pause.)

JAKE. *(Slightly annoyed.) Yes*, I can lift / them –

CHRIS. Don't get pissy, I just meant with the –

JAKE. *I'm fine.*

CHRIS. Okay, good then.

(He moves to one side of one of the televisions, motions for **JAKE** *to move to the other side. They lift the box, moving it to the shelf.)*

JAKE. Look I didn't tell her that we were together, she / just assumed –

CHRIS. Okay, I'd *really* prefer that we didn't talk about this / right now –

JAKE. And I'm sorry about the Iowa thing, I had no idea she didn't know. Seriously, you told me like the first day I met you, I didn't think it was some big –...

(Pause.)

I just wanted to tell her that you still cared about her, that's all I was trying to do. I was just trying to help.

> *(They move the television to the shelf.* **CHRIS** *stands on the palette, pushing the box to the back to make room for more.)*

CHRIS. Look can we just work, okay? How about we just work.

JAKE. Okay.

> *(They go to another television, lifting it.)*

CHRIS. *(Quiet.)* She knows that I [care about her] –.

JAKE. What?

CHRIS. I said *she knows that I care about her.* You just have no idea what you're –. You don't know what it's like.

> *(They put the television on the shelf.* **CHRIS** *shoves it to the back.)*

JAKE. Look, I can imagine this must be hard.

> *(***CHRIS** *stops working, looks at* **JAKE***.)*

CHRIS. I worked all through high school, full-time during the summer and after school during the year, to save up for college. Second half of my senior year, she got ahold of my account and blew through all of it in three months. When I was a junior in college, I almost flunked out of a Comp Lit class because she sold my laptop the day before my final paper was due.

> *(Pause.)*

When I was fourteen, she kicked me out of the house for six days when I flushed her stash. I was so embarrassed I didn't tell anyone, so I slept in the parking lot behind the mall.

> *(Pause. They look at one another.)*

> *(After a moment,* **CHRIS** *looks back at the boxes, about to pick up another one. Before he can bend down to get it,* **JAKE** *goes to him, his arms outstretched.)*

CHRIS. Jake, no no no no –

> (*JAKE wraps his arms around* **CHRIS**, *embracing him.*)
>
> (*It's awkward at first,* **CHRIS** *is tense and looking around to make sure no one is watching. But after a moment he relaxes into it, accepts it.*)
>
> (*They hug for a moment longer, then* **JAKE** *releases him.* **CHRIS** *looks away, goes back to the boxes.*)

JAKE. Has she ever like gotten *help*, or –?

CHRIS. She doesn't think she needs help.

> (*Pause.* **JAKE** *goes to the box, lifts the other side. They put it on the shelf.* **CHRIS** *softens a little.*)

I mean it's –. It's been better lately, she's clean now.

JAKE. That's good.

> (*Pause.*)

Has she –? I mean has she been clean before?

CHRIS. A few times. I told her if she used again then she was out of my life for good.

JAKE. Did you mean it?

> (*Pause.*)

CHRIS. Probably not. I've said it before.

> (*Pause.*)
>
> (*He bends down to get another box.* **JAKE** *grabs the other end, they put it on the shelf.*)

She told me yesterday she wants us to move away.

> (*Pause.*)

JAKE. What do you mean?

CHRIS. Like she wants me to leave town with her, move somewhere else. Make a fresh start.

> (*Pause.*)

JAKE. You're going to move with her?

CHRIS. I don't know. She said if I went with her she'd go into a program. Maybe she'll actually do it this time, I don't know. It'd probably be good for her to get out of town.

(Pause.)

JAKE. What about grad school?

CHRIS. Whatever, I can apply some other year.

(He bends down to get a box, waits for **JAKE** *to lift the other end.* **JAKE** *doesn't move; he looks at* **CHRIS**.*)*

What?

JAKE. Chris, you can't –. You're really gonna do that?

CHRIS. Why not? Nothing's keeping me here.

JAKE. You have a life here.

CHRIS. Not much of one. Plus she needs someone to take care of her, no one else is gonna do it. Are you gonna [lift this with me] –?

(Pause.)

JAKE. You realize that you're just her enabler, right?

*(***CHRIS** *stands up, looking at* **JAKE**.*)*

CHRIS. Excuse me?

JAKE. You're just –. I mean you tell her that if she uses again then you're gonna leave her for good, but then she uses again and you just forgive her, it's just –. You're just allowing her to keep doing this.

(Pause. **CHRIS** *bends down, grabbing another box.)*

CHRIS. Lift it.

JAKE. Chris.

CHRIS. You gonna do your job or not?

JAKE. Look I'm not trying to be a jerk, but if you're gonna tell me how terrible your life is, then I'm going to like try to offer you *solutions* –

(**CHRIS** *stands up, looking at him.*)

CHRIS. Okay, you're starting to piss me off.

JAKE. I'm just saying, if you're gonna tell her that she's gonna be out of your life then you should *mean* it, and not –. Now she wants you to move away with her, so you can just like *attend* to her addiction in some other town –

CHRIS. Stop acting like you give a fuck about my mom. You're just mad because you think I'm your boyfriend and you don't want me to leave.

(*Pause.*)

JAKE. That is / *not true* –

CHRIS. But actually, Jake, I'm *not* your boyfriend, and I won't ever be, so / maybe –

JAKE. I do *not* think that you're my / boyfriend –

CHRIS. Well you told my mom that you were.

JAKE. *I did not tell her that she just / assumed* –

CHRIS. And by the way, I think the whole reason you came here is sort of pathetic.

(*Silence. He stares at* **JAKE**.)

JAKE. What?

CHRIS. I mean so you're like *barely* related to William Clark, who fucking cares? Clark was just some asshole imperialist who wrote some journals and drew some stupid maps, walked across the country just so we could have more shitty fucking towns like this one.

JAKE. Chris, / stop it –

CHRIS. And you come out here, and you can't even fucking *drive* all the way to the ocean without breaking down and threatening to kill yourself to some *stranger*, it's so fucking [pathetic] –...

(*Pause.*)

I don't even know why you're still here. Are you just sticking around so you can mess with my personal life?

(Pause.)

Why the fuck are you still here, Jake?

JAKE. Chris, please –

CHRIS. You know what? I don't even care. I don't even know you, I don't care. We're co-workers and that's it, I don't know why I even –. Lift the other side.

(Pause. He goes for another box.)

JAKE. Chris...

*(**CHRIS** goes to **JAKE**, looking at him.)*

CHRIS. I don't care. I don't care about you.

(Pause.)

Lift the fucking box.

*(He goes back to the box. He looks at **JAKE**, waiting for him to lift.)*

*(**JAKE**, upset and not knowing what to do, goes to the other side of the box.)*

JAKE. Chris, *please.*

*(**CHRIS** doesn't respond to him. They lift the box.)*

*(Just as the box is almost on the shelf, **JAKE** suddenly drops his end. The box crashes to the floor; a large shattering sound is heard.)*

*(**CHRIS** looks at the box, horrified. He looks at **JAKE**. **JAKE** stares back at him.)*

Oops.

(They stare at one another.)

Scene Nine

(The parking lot, later. **JAKE** *holds his cell phone. He looks at it for a moment, then makes a call.)*

JAKE. Hi, Dad, I'm –. I woke you up, I'm sorry, it's –.

(Pause.)

Yeah, I'm fine, I –... Actually, no, I'm not fine. No, it's not that, I'm taking my meds, I'm safe. And I'm –. I'm sorry for leaving like that, I know that wasn't fair of me, I know it was stupid, but I guess I –...

(Pause. He looks out toward the river.)

Dad, I'm – in Washington.

(Pause.)

No, the state. Eastern Washington, near the Idaho border.

(Pause.)

Yeah, it's –. It's near the trail. I'm actually looking over it right now, it's – kinda beautiful. I mean it's – you know – it's just a little town, I'm standing in a parking lot, but. I don't know, I still think it's sort of beautiful, there's something –...

(Pause. He looks away from the river, staring at the ground.)

I sound – so dumb. I hear that now.

(Pause.)

I guess – I've been trying to be a different person. The kind of person I've always wanted to be. But I'm kidding myself, I'm not that guy. I'm just a stranger here. And – I need to grow up.

(Pause.)

I know I can just come home. I know.

(He continues to stare at the asphalt.)

Scene Ten

(The parking lot, shortly later, nearing dawn. **JAKE** *stands with his backpack, waiting anxiously. After a moment,* **CHRIS** *enters. He stops, looks at* **JAKE**.*)*

JAKE. Look I told Janet it was my fault, I told her I wasn't up front about having Huntington's, and –. Look I took the blame, she let me go and we're –

CHRIS. I got fired.

(Pause.)

We destroyed a five-thousand-dollar television, Jake. We *both* got fired.

JAKE. But that's not –! I told her it was my fault!

CHRIS. Well since I knew you were sick and I didn't say anything, Janet says that I'm still partially to / blame –

JAKE. You told her that?

CHRIS. I said that I had been covering for you and / that you –

JAKE. Chris, why did you tell her that? You didn't / need to –

CHRIS. Well I didn't think I was gonna be fucking *questioned* today, Jake, I didn't fucking *prepare* my *story* –

JAKE. I'm sorry, I –. I'm just sorry.

(Pause.)

Look, I'm gonna go talk to Janet –

(He starts for the Costco, **CHRIS** *blocks him.)*

CHRIS. It's done. I'm fired.

(Pause.)

You just got me fired.

(Silence. He stares at **JAKE**. **JAKE** *is at a loss.)*

You did that on purpose.

(Silence. They stare at one another.)

JAKE. I was mad.

CHRIS. You fucking / asshole.

JAKE. Look you were being really hurtful, and I didn't know / what to do –

CHRIS. Do you even *know* how much five thousand dollars is?

> *(Pause.)*

JAKE. What?

CHRIS. That TV you just broke cost five thousand dollars, and what really pisses me off is I don't think you know how much that is. I think – if you needed five thousand dollars? I think you could call up Mommy or Daddy and they would send you five thousand dollars. I think for you five thousand dollars is pretty much meaningless.

JAKE. I know / how much –

CHRIS. Do you know what five thousand dollars is to *me*? Five thousand dollars is what I can put toward my college loans after *eighteen months* of working *full-time.* That's what five thousand dollars means to me. And in your fucking childlike *tantrum*, you *threw it away.*

> *(**JAKE** sits down on the pavement, his head in his hands.)*

JAKE. I'm sorry.

CHRIS. Are you?

JAKE. I'm fucked up.

CHRIS. *(Exasperated.) Jesus –*

JAKE. I'm really fucked up, Chris, I know I am.

> *(Silence. **CHRIS** paces.)*

CHRIS. What are you doing here, Jake? Why did you come here, why did you start working here?

JAKE. I just –…

> *(Pause.)*

I just wanted to do the Lewis and Clark Trail, to follow it to the ocean – just do this one *last thing* before the

Huntington's got really bad. I didn't even tell my mom or my dad what I was doing, I just left, got in my car, but by the time I got out here, I –...

(Pause.)

I couldn't make it.

CHRIS. Why?

JAKE. I almost drove off the road.

(Pause.)

When I was coming down the grade into town, I almost... I lost control of my leg and I couldn't hit the brake, I –... I went up one of those runaway truck ramps, if it had lasted a second longer I probably would have –...

(Pause.)

I barely got into town, pulled into the first hotel I saw. And I realized that the Costco was right across the street, and I thought I could just – work there for a while, do something *real*, wait for the chorea to get better –...

(Pause. He looks at **CHRIS**.)

I drove out here in *four days*. That's how long it took me. In my nice car with my air-conditioning, stopping for bathroom breaks and Red Bulls and –. I realized I've never really had to do anything difficult in my entire life. The one thing I set out to do, to come out here, see the ocean? All I had to do was sit behind a wheel for a few days. And I couldn't even do that. I couldn't even fucking make it.

(Pause.)

The chorea is getting worse. Yesterday I tried to drive across the bridge, just to get to the spot where Lewis and Clark were camping... I was too scared to leave the parking lot. I feel like I'm fucking *trapped* here.

(Pause. **CHRIS** paces.)

CHRIS. This is –. This is *really shitty* of you, you know? I mean you got me *fired* today and now it's like I'm not even allowed to get mad at you because you're –...

> *(Pause.)*

Fuck.

> *(Pause.)*

JAKE. I'm sorry –

CHRIS. Jake, did you –? You really thought coming out west was a *solution*, you really thought that it would –...? I don't know what kind of magical pioneer land you expected, but this is just some stupid town, it's just –...

> *(Pause.)*

Look you need to understand something. *I can't help you*. Okay? Ever since you came here I feel like you're like asking me for some solution to your problems, but *I don't have it*. My life is pretty shitty right now too, if I knew how to make it better don't you think I would have done it?

JAKE. I'm sorry. I don't deserve your help. I'm sorry.

> *(Pause.)*

CHRIS. Look, just –. Have you talked to your mom or dad?

> *(Pause.)*

JAKE. I've talked to my dad a few times.

CHRIS. Well just *tell* him, tell him where you are, tell him to buy you a plane ticket or whatever, and *go home*. Okay?

> *(**JAKE** looks up. He stands up, looking at the river.)*

JAKE. Yeah I –.

> *(Pause.)*

I guess that's what's gonna happen.

> *(Pause. **CHRIS** watches him.)*

> *(**TRISHA** enters.)*

CHRIS. Mom, what're you –?

TRISHA. You got off early! Thought I'd be waiting around for an hour.

(Pause.)

You okay?

(Pause.)

CHRIS. We got fired.

(Pause.)

TRISHA. *Both* of you?

CHRIS. We broke a TV. A very big, very expensive / TV.

JAKE. *I* broke it, it was my [fault] –.

(Pause.)

It was my fault.

(Pause.)

TRISHA. You know what? This is a good thing, this is perfect timing.

*(**CHRIS** looks at her.)*

CHRIS. What –?

TRISHA. You remember Melanie?

CHRIS. Melanie?

TRISHA. Yeah, three-four years ago, she stayed with us for a while?

CHRIS. Wait, the –. She was married to the biker guy, the / one who –?

TRISHA. Divorced him three months ago. Best thing that's ever happened to her, really turned her life / around –

CHRIS. Mom, you told me you / wouldn't hang out with –

TRISHA. Outta nowhere yesterday she sends me a text, says she's in town, so I got together with her after work. She's out in Missoula now, she's living in this house with a couple other gals, you might remember one of them. Point is, I was talkin' to her about Missoula – you remember, we went there once when you were a kid, you remember?

CHRIS. No, I don't –

TRISHA. You were little, but I bet you'd remember if you saw it, it's so beautiful, and the people are just so nice, and *that's* where we can go! We could find work there just as easy as we could around here. I'm ready to up and leave, seriously. Already told Gary that I'm not gonna be in the apartment next month. Told him he can keep the security deposit, I don't care, use the money to pay someone to haul all the furniture out of there to the dump –

JAKE. *(Moving to exit.)* I can let you guys [talk] –

TRISHA. *(To* **JAKE.***)* You wanna come with us?

> *(***JAKE*** stops.)*

JAKE. What?

TRISHA. Fuck it, why not? You got fired too, yeah? I mean I don't know how much room Melanie's got in the house, but I bet you could find work out there just as easy as you could here.

> *(***JAKE*** *looks at* ***CHRIS.*** ***CHRIS*** *stares at* ***TRISHA.***)*

JAKE. I –... I mean I / don't –

CHRIS. Mom.

TRISHA. She's there in this house with a couple other gals I know you've met one of them a while back, her name's Lydia, she has this big red hair, you'll remember her. And the mountains are so pretty, these big mountains / and the –

CHRIS. You're high.

> *(Silence.)*

TRISHA. What?

CHRIS. You used.

> *(Pause.)*

Mom, are you high right now?

TRISHA. No!

CHRIS. *Are you high right now?*

TRISHA. Chris I am *not* / high –

CHRIS. Tell me.

> *(Pause.)*

TRISHA. Chris –

CHRIS. *Tell me right now.*

> *(Pause.)*

TRISHA. Look I'm coming down off it already, Melanie and I just did a little bump, it's no big deal.

> (**CHRIS**' *head falls into his chest.*)

Now okay don't –. Now don't make this into some big *thing*, this isn't like before. Melanie just had this little bit left. She's going cold turkey after this, and we just –. Okay it was dumb of me, but it's not like before, this was just us having some fun.

> (**CHRIS** *goes to the ground, sitting on the asphalt, his head buried in his hands.*)

CHRIS. *Why?*

TRISHA. Chris, I'm sorry, I know I screwed up – but seriously it was just this little bit and I'm already comin' down off it, so just calm down. No big deal.

> *(She gets down on the ground, putting her arms around him.)*

CHRIS. Mom.

TRISHA. Okay, now *stop it*, you don't need to –… I'm not going back to my old habits, this was just one little –. *(To* **JAKE**.*)* Do I look like a junkie to you?

> (**JAKE** *is frozen, unsure of what to do.*)

JAKE. I –. I mean I / don't –

TRISHA. C'mon, do I look like some addict / who –

CHRIS. *Please. Stop.*

> (**TRISHA** *hugs* **CHRIS** *tighter.*)

TRISHA. Okay, let's just focus on the good stuff, okay? Let's focus on getting ourselves outta Clarkston.

(Pause.)

TRISHA. Listen why don't we run by your place, we can grab whatever you wanna take?

(Silence.)

*(***CHRIS*** finally looks up. He looks at **TRISHA**. She smiles at him. He looks at **JAKE**, then back at **TRISHA**.)*

C'mon. Let's go get your stuff –

CHRIS. I can't see you again?

*(Pause. **TRISHA** looks at him.)*

TRISHA. What?

CHRIS. I can't see you again.

(Pause.)

I can't see you again.

*(Pause. **TRISHA** stands up.)*

*(***CHRIS*** looks up at her.)*

I told you if you used again then you were out of my life –

TRISHA. What're you / saying?

CHRIS. I can't do this anymore.

(Pause.)

I'm sorry. I can't do this anymore.

*(***TRISHA*** stares at him, shocked.)*

TRISHA. Look, I get it, okay?! I screwed up! I shouldn't have done that, I get it!

*(***CHRIS*** looks away from her, staring at the ground. Pause.)*

Chris, I'm going to Missoula right now, with or without you. You don't have a job here, you don't have anything, nothing's keeping you here. We're a team, we've been through worse than this. Let's just *go*.

(Pause.)

Chris. Let's go.

> *(CHRIS doesn't move, he continues to stare at the ground. JAKE turns away, uncomfortable but feeling compelled to stay with CHRIS.)*
>
> *(TRISHA looks at CHRIS. The reality of the situation slowly begins to dawn on her.)*
>
> *(Silence.)*

So what, you're *giving up* on me? Is that what you're doing?

> *(Pause.)*

You know there were a lot of times I could of given up on you, you realize that? You think Dad left because I was getting *high*? He left two weeks after he found out you were gay. We've all got our demons, Chris, I accepted yours.

> *(CHRIS lies down on the asphalt, curling up into the fetal position, facing upstage. TRISHA bears down on him, shouting:)*

FINE, I DON'T NEED YOU. STAY HERE WITH YOUR FUCKIN' *BOYFRIEND*, YOUR –.

> *(She stops herself, taking a few breaths. She looks at JAKE, who continues to look away. Silence. She turns to leave.)*

I'm done, to hell with this.

> *(She stops, turns back to CHRIS, her anger dissolved into a deep sadness.)*
>
> *(Silence.)*

(Pleading.) Chris, please.

> *(Pause.)*

Christopher.

> *(Pause.)*

TRISHA. Christopher.

> *(Pause.)*

Chris.

> *(**CHRIS** doesn't move. **TRISHA** looks at him for a moment longer, then finally turns and exits. After a moment we hear the sound of a car door shutting, an engine starting, a car driving off.)*
>
> *(Silence.)*
>
> *(**JAKE** looks at **CHRIS**, who remains curled up, facing upstage. **JAKE** cautiously approaches him.)*
>
> *(Finally:)*

JAKE. Chris.

> *(Pause.)*

She's gone, Chris.

> *(**CHRIS** doesn't move. **JAKE** looks down on him, not knowing what to say.)*

I don't –. I don't want to leave you.

> *(Pause.)*

Is it okay if I don't leave you?

> *(Pause. **CHRIS** doesn't respond. **JAKE** paces.)*

You know, maybe this is all like –. I mean maybe this is a good thing. For both of you. I mean in a few months you might be getting your MFA out in Iowa, spending your days writing / stories and –

CHRIS. I didn't get in.

> *(Pause.)*

JAKE. What?

CHRIS. I got a rejection letter. Two days ago.

> *(Pause.)*

JAKE. Oh.

(*Pause.*)

Well look I mean there's like waitlists, and –

CHRIS. I didn't get waitlisted. I got rejected. It was a form letter.

(*Pause.*)

It came early. Which means I got rejected in the first round.

(*Pause.* **JAKE** *cautiously sits down on the ground next to* **CHRIS**.)

(**JAKE** *reaches over to put a hand on* **CHRIS***' shoulder, but stops himself. He looks out to the river, trying to think of what to say.*)

JAKE. I'll just sit with you. I'll sit with you for a while. Is that okay?

(*Pause.* **CHRIS** *doesn't respond.* **JAKE** *continues to watch the river.*)

Okay.

(*Pause.*)

Can I read another one of your stories? I could read it out loud?

CHRIS. *No.*

JAKE. Okay, sorry, I –.

(*Silence.*)

(*Finally,* **JAKE** *opens his backpack, taking out the book from before.*)

I can read you some more from the journals? You wanna hear some more?

(*Pause.* **CHRIS** *doesn't respond.*)

(**JAKE** *opens up the book, flips a few pages.*)

August 24, 1804.

"One evidence which the Indians give for believing this place to be the residence of some unusual spirits is that they frequently discover a large assemblage of birds

around this mound – is in my opinion a sufficient proof
to produce in the savage mind a confident belief of –"

(Stops, flips pages.)

Okay maybe something less racist maybe. Okay – May
15, 1805.

"We saw buffalo on the banks dead, others floating
down dead, and others mired every day, those buffalo
either drown in swimming the river or –"

(Stops reading.)

Okay let's just –. Let's just get them to the ocean, maybe
that'll be more optimistic.

(He flips a few pages, landing on something.)

Okay here.

"Great joy in camp. We are now in view of the ocean,
this great Pacific Ocean which we have been so long
anxious to see. And the roaring or noise made by the
waves breaking on the rocky shores, as I suppose, may
be heard distinctly. We made thirty-four miles today as
computed.

(Pause.)

"Notwithstanding the disagreeable time of the party
for several days past, they are all cheerful and full of
anxiety to see further into the ocean. The water is too
salt to drink, we use rain water.

*(CHRIS lifts himself up slightly off the ground,
pulling himself toward JAKE, still facing
upstage. He rests his head in JAKE's lap. JAKE
watches him for a moment, then goes back to
reading.)*

"November 19, 1805. I arose early this morning from
under a wet blanket caused by a shower of rain which
fell in the latter part of the last night, and sent two
men on ahead with directions to proceed on near the
sea coast and kill something for breakfast. After drying
our blankets a little I set out with a view to proceed

near the coast. The bay was at no great distance across. I overtook the hunters at about three miles, they had killed a small deer on which we had breakfast.

(Pause. He raises his hand, considers placing it on the side of **CHRIS**' *head. He stops, puts it down.)*

"After taking a sumptuous breakfast of venison –"

CHRIS. "Sumptuous"? It says that?

(Pause.)

JAKE. Yeah.

CHRIS. That's funny.

JAKE. Yeah.

(He gently puts his hand on **CHRIS**' *head as he reads.)*

"After taking a sumptuous breakfast of venison which was roasted on sticks exposed to the fire, I proceeded on through rugged country of high hills and steep hollers on a course from the cape, north twenty degrees west, five miles on a direct line to the commencement of a sandy coast which extended north ten degrees west from the top of the hill above the sand shore to a point of high land distant near twenty miles. This point I have taken the liberty of calling after my particular friend Lewis.

*(***CHRIS** *rolls over, facing downstage, his head still in* **JAKE**'s *lap. He watches the river.)*

"I proceeded on the sandy coast four miles, and marked my name on a small pine, the day of the month and year, etc., and returned to the foot of this hill, from which place I intended to strike across the Bay. I saw a sturgeon which had been thrown on shore and left by the tide ten feet in length, and several joints of the backbone of a whale which must have been foundered on –"

CHRIS. They camped right over there?

*(**JAKE** looks up, across the river, to where **CHRIS** is looking. Pause.)*

JAKE. Yeah. Right over there.

(Silence.)

CHRIS. That's neat.

(Pause. They look over the river.)

Scene Eleven

(Several weeks later.)

(For the first time, the space feels open, bright, and natural. The sound of the river has been replaced by the sound of ocean waves crashing against a rocky shoreline.

(CHRIS *and* **JAKE** *sit together on the sand, barefoot, wearing jackets.)*

(Silence as they look over the ocean.)

JAKE. Is it what you expected?

CHRIS. I guess. I mean I've seen pictures so it's not too surprising. It's nice.

(Pause.)

JAKE. Thanks for driving me out here.

CHRIS. Sure. I've never seen it either.

(Silence. They look for a moment longer, then **CHRIS** *starts to get up.)*

You ready?

*(***JAKE** *looks at him.)*

JAKE. What, you're *done*?

CHRIS. Yeah?

JAKE. We've been here for like ten minutes.

CHRIS. I mean we've *seen* it, so.

JAKE. It took us *eight hours* to drive here and you wanna leave after ten minutes?!

*(***CHRIS** *looks out to the ocean.)*

CHRIS. I like it, it's nice! It's just –. I mean there it is, I've seen it. It's what I expected it to look like, it's what it looks like in the photographs.

JAKE. Oh my God I don't understand you.

CHRIS. Look I just don't want to be driving in the dark / and we –

*(**JAKE** stands up.)*

JAKE. Okay, stop. It's the Fourth of July, it's your day off, relax for Christ's sake. Just – look.

(They both look out to the ocean.)

CHRIS. Yeah?

JAKE. I mean think what it was like for Lewis and Clark when they got here, and they *hadn't* seen a photograph. It was just all – *new.*

CHRIS. It must have been awesome. But I *have* seen a photograph of it so –

JAKE. Yeah I'm asking you to fucking pretend. Pretend like you're seeing all this for the first time.

(They both look out to the ocean.)

CHRIS. I mean it's nice.

*(**JAKE** sighs, exasperated.)*

What?!

JAKE. Never mind.

(Pause.)

Well I think it's –. I've never seen it and I think it's pretty amazing. I feel like I'm seeing it for the first time, and it's –

*(He has a sudden involuntary movement in his leg, he grabs it. **CHRIS** watches him.)*

*(**JAKE** takes a few deep breaths.)*

CHRIS. You okay?

JAKE. Yeah, I just –.

(Pause.)

I really hate this.

CHRIS. I know.

*(Pause. **JAKE** punches his leg in frustration, **CHRIS** goes to him.)*

Okay, okay –

(Silence. **JAKE** *looks out to the ocean.* **CHRIS** *watches him.)*

JAKE. You know what's really weird? I've actually never been able to picture myself getting old.

(Pause.)

CHRIS. What do you mean?

JAKE. I mean even when I was little, I –. I could picture myself being a teenager, I could picture myself being in my twenties, but I –. I just could never picture myself actually –. I guess somewhere in my brain I've always known I wouldn't live very long.

(Pause.)

It's like – I should be having some big revelation now, some epiphany about what to do with the years that I have left, but I –. I don't.

(Pause.)

Do you think that makes me a pathetic person?

(Pause. **CHRIS** *goes to him.)*

CHRIS. Don't be so hard on yourself? You're not dying tomorrow. And I'll be around, you know.

JAKE. For a while. Until you get into grad school somewhere, move away, start getting old.

(Pause.)

I guess I have no idea what's in front of me. That feels new, at least.

(Pause. He looks out to the ocean for a moment, then takes out his iPhone.)

Here, you want your picture with the ocean in the background?

CHRIS. Oh, no.

(Pause. **JAKE** *looks at him.)*

JAKE. You don't / want your –?

CHRIS. I mean I just don't want it to be a whole *thing*, like you take a photo and post it to Facebook and people comment / on it and –

JAKE. I won't post it to Facebook, oh my God.

CHRIS. I also just –. I don't like having my picture taken.

JAKE. Okay we'll take it together.

(He stands next to **CHRIS**.*)*

CHRIS. Jake, c'mon –

JAKE. Shut up I hate you.

(He fiddles with his iPhone, turning the camera on. He swaps the screen so that the front-facing camera is turned on.)

Here, you have longer arms.

(He gives the phone to **CHRIS**, *who reluctantly takes it. They stand next to one another, facing upstage.* **CHRIS** *holds up the phone so we see their faces on the screen. He snaps a quick photo.)*

CHRIS. There.

(He gives the phone to **JAKE**.*)*

JAKE. *(Looking at the photo.)* Oof, no. Take it again.

CHRIS. *Jake.*

JAKE. You look like an *ogre* in this photo. You look like you're going to go eat some babies.

CHRIS. Shut up gimme the [phone] –.

(He takes the phone again. They pose again for the shot. **CHRIS** *raises the phone.)*

JAKE. Relax!

(He puts an arm around **CHRIS**. **CHRIS** *relaxes, smiles a bit. He takes a photo of the two of them, gives the phone to* **JAKE**. **JAKE** *looks at it.)*

There. It's nice! See?

(He hands the phone to **CHRIS**, *who looks at it.)*

(Silence.)

What?

*(***CHRIS*** *doesn't respond, still looking at the photo.)*

You okay?

CHRIS. Yeah, I –.

(Pause. He looks at the photo. He takes a few steps toward the water.)

I'm just realizing – I think up until this second I never thought I'd see the ocean.

(Pause.)

I didn't realize that I thought that.

(Pause. **JAKE** *takes a few steps forward, joining* **CHRIS**.*)*

(They continue to look out to the ocean.)

End of Play

www.ingramcontent.com/pod-product-compliance
Lightning Source LLC
Chambersburg PA
CBHW071924130726
47909CB00014B/2566